EAT HIM IF YOU LIKE

Jean Teulé lives in the Marais with his companion, the French film actress Miou-Miou. An illustrator, filmmaker and television presenter, he is also the prize-winning author of eleven books including *The Suicide Shop*.

Emily Phillips studied French and Spanish at the University of Bath. She lives and works in Bristol.

Praise for *Eat Him if You Like*

'This gripping and gory short novel revisits one of French history's stranger episodes… Jean Teulé's novelisation offers no easy explanations for what happened, but the transformation from rural idyll to hell on earth is terrifyingly convincing.'
Financial Times

'Teulé's hard-hitting account is shattering. In holding up a mirror to the murderous capacity of ordinary people, he has produced an extraordinary novel.'
Paris Match

'With his customary verve… Jean Teulé tells in terrifying detail the story of the poor boy's calvary, as he passes from surprise to incomprehension, then terror, resignation and, finally, forgiveness.'
Madame Figaro

EAT HIM IF YOU LIKE

Also by Jean Teulé :

The Suicide Shop
Monsieur Montespan

EAT HIM IF YOU LIKE

A NOVEL BY
JEAN TEULÉ

TRANSLATED FROM THE FRENCH BY
EMILY PHILLIPS

GALLIC BOOKS
London

This book is published with support from the French Ministry of Culture/
Centre national du Livre

Liberté • Égalité • Fraternité
RÉPUBLIQUE FRANÇAISE

A Gallic Book

First published in France as Mangez-le si vous voulez by Éditions Julliard,
Paris
Copyright Éditions Julliard Paris, 2009

First published in Great Britain in 2011 by Gallic Books, 134 Lots Road,
London SW10 0RJ

A CIP record for this book is available from the British Library

ISBN 978-1-906040-39-0

Typeset in Fournier by Gallic Books
Printed and bound by CPI Group (UK) Ltd, Croydon, CR0 4YY

2 4 6 8 10 9 7 5 3 1

1

THE BRETANGES ESTATE

'What a beautiful day!' declared the young man, pushing open his bedroom shutters. Muslin curtains fluttered on either side of the upstairs window of the seventeenth-century house. His gaze swept the countryside – a small corner of Limousin attached to Périgord as if by mistake. The parched landscape was dotted with oak trees. A clock struck one on the mantelpiece behind him.

'What time do you call this? And you the new deputy mayor of Beaussac! When I was mayor, I got up much earlier!' boomed a deep voice from under the ancient chestnut tree in the garden.

'Father, I was putting the finishing touches to my project to divert the Nizonne.'

'Amédée,' said a woman's voice from the shade of the tree, 'stop badgering our son. At least he's dressed. You look good in your summer suit, Alain,' continued his mother, fanning herself. 'Don't forget your boater, it's another scorcher today,'

Alain grabbed his straw hat from the rosewood table and went downstairs. The dark staircase smelt strongly of wax polish and the tap of his soft leather boots on the stairs betrayed a slight limp. An old, worn tapestry hung in the entrance hall. Alain paused in front of a framed picture depicting the main square of a small, deserted market town.

'You like that picture of Hautefaye, don't you?' exclaimed his mother, watching him through the open front door.

'Yes, I do. Our neighbours are so friendly,' replied Alain, leaving the house to join his parents who were sitting at the garden table about to have lunch. 'I hope my drainage project will be approved and I hope they'll all like it, as they did in Beaussac.'

'You slept so late I thought you'd forgotten about the fair,' muttered his father, his nose in the local paper.

'Father, I've never missed the Hautefaye fair. All my friends will be there.' Alain went over to embrace his mother, a dark-haired woman with blue eyes.

'Oh, you're such a wonderful boy, so helpful and uncomplicated. You were born to please, always smiling, always with an angelic look in your eyes,' she gushed, stroking his cheek.

His father rolled his eyes, uncomfortable with this

excessive display of motherly love. Alain moved into the shade of the chestnut tree.

'It's so beautifully cool under here. Perfect on such a hot, muggy day. It's as though it were put here for this very purpose.'

'Well, stay under the tree then, instead of going to war,' said his mother, anxious all of a sudden. 'Dear Lord, you'll be in Lorraine next week fighting in this wretched war against Prussia. Why must you go when the medical board has already exempted you for having a weak constitution? Do you want me to die of worry? You could easily have exchanged your unlucky conscription number at Pons when you were in Périgueux. It would only have cost us a thousand francs. Alain, are you listening to me?'

'Magdeleine-Louise, he's already told you hundreds of times!' said his father in exasperation. 'He doesn't approve of a lottery to decide who goes to war. Especially because poor boys who draw a lucky ticket then sell it to wealthy boys who have an unlucky one.'

'Mother, everybody knows and likes me here in Nontron, and I would be so ashamed if I came across the parents of the boy who'd gone to fight in my place . . . Anyway, my limp won't be a problem, as I'll be in the cavalry.'

Alain shouted over to the household servant, who was dozing under an arbour, 'Pascal, would you saddle my horse, please?'

'Aren't you eating with us?' asked his mother, surprised. 'Look, we've got lentils with bacon and that soft cheese you like.'

'No, I'll have lunch at the fair, at Mousnier's inn. I'm

meeting the Marthon notary there.'

'Why?' asked his father.

'Before going to the front, I need to sort out some estate business. I promised to give our poor neighbour, old Bertille, a heifer to replace the cow that drowned in the Nizonne marshes. I also said I would help the farmer at Lac Noir re-roof his barn. It was hit by lightning in last week's storm and I want to try and find a carpenter in Hautefaye who'll be able to start working on it as soon as possible. I was thinking of Pierre Brut, that roofer from Fayemarteau. It's urgent and I'll have to make the necessary arrangements before I leave for Lorraine.'

Alain paused at the edge of the meadow to listen to the hornets buzzing and the cicadas chirring. A pretty little lark broke into song and then flew from its perch on a dry bush.

'My head's spinning,' said his mother, who was feeling unwell. Already suffering from poor health, she was badly affected by her son's enlistment.

'It's the heat, Mother.'

'What does the paper say, my boy? Does it mention Prussia? Did we beat them at Reichshoffen and Forbach? I don't have my glasses.'

Alain picked up the *Dordogne Echo*, which was lying beside his father's plate. His father was looking at it but said nothing.

'Is this really today's paper?' he asked. 'Tuesday 16 August 1870. Ah yes, this is it.'

Shocked by the headlines, he decided only to read out a small column from the bottom of the front page:

'The drought continues unabated and the situation is going from bad to worse. Larger towns are already rationing water and, in some areas, citizens are to receive no more than eight pints per person per day. In areas that have no large springs or streams, people are travelling long distances to the nearest river or are having to pay for water.'

'It is rather hot,' agreed his mother.

'Why don't you go and play the piano in the drawing room after lunch? You'll feel cooler in there.'

Pascal brought over Alain's fine chestnut horse and held out the reins to him. As Alain mounted, his mother advised him to return before nightfall.

'Mother, I'm almost thirty! And Hautefaye is only two miles away. I'll just go there, say hello to a few people and come straight back. See you later.'

2

THE ROAD TO THE FAIR

Alain's thoughts wandered as he travelled along, dreaming, carefree, and revelling happily in his surroundings. His horse's mane rose and fell in gentle waves as they trotted along. Vine-covered slopes bordered the dusty, well-worn track, and the sun was striving to sweeten and swell the grapes. The oppressive heat had even silenced the cicadas. Alain's eyelids drooped and he began to daydream.

He opened his eyes again and saw a stream of traders, labourers and artisans ahead of him on the dirt track. They resembled a flock of geese as they converged on the fair, some on foot, and others riding donkeys, or driving carts. Alain squeezed past on the right, overtaking two farmers from Mainzac.

'Good day, Étienne Campot. How are you, Jean?' he said, greeting them.

'Good day to you, Monsieur de Monéys,' said the Campot brothers, doffing their caps in their usual polite manner. Étienne must have been around the same age as Alain. Jean was about twenty, with a mane of unruly hair. The elder of the two was leading a large horse.

'Whoa, Jupiter!'

'Why are you bringing your fine dray horse to the fair, lads?'

'We're hoping to sell him to the army. They don't have enough horses and the army suppliers sometimes come to fairs to buy mounts for the Lorraine front.'

'So both of our horses will face the Prussians then, Étienne! I have offered to take my chestnut with me when I enlist, and afterwards I'll leave him to the army.'

'You're going to war, Monsieur de Monéys? What about your gammy leg?' asked Jean, surprised. 'Weren't you able to swap your unlucky number?'

'The Besse boy offered to take my place, but I refused. In three days' time I'll be off to fight for my country.'

'Where will you be stationed?'

'I'm still awaiting my marching orders. Did you get lucky numbers?'

'Yes, thankfully we both did,' sighed the elder Campot brother gratefully. He was an intelligent, warm-hearted man with a moustache, a wide forehead and big eyes. His eyes filled with tears as he looked at Jupiter, who would soon be going to war. He clenched his fists and tried to think of something else.

Alain overtook a few small, exhausted donkeys laden with ripe-smelling melons, and a crowd of artisans from neighbouring parishes.

'I like to dance like there's no tomorrow!' declared one of them, a stonemason who was talking about love, happiness and pleasure.

The plain was as dry as a bone. As Alain continued

continued on his way, he was surrounded by goodwill. Flowers of friendship blossomed in his path, and he was met by shouts of 'Good day, Monsieur de Monéys', 'How are you, Alain? And is your mother well?' François Mazière, a farmer from Plambaut, close to Hautefaye, was telling a man he had come to sell his two bullocks. From time to time, he chivvied them along in patois. '*Aqui bloundo! Aqui! Véqué!*'

Alain knew the man who was walking beside him as well. He was a jocular middle aged ragman. He and his small donkey that travelled everywhere with him would go to the farms in Nontron and collect all the tattered clothes and rags. Sometimes people gave them to him for free and sometimes he had to pay a small price. He would then bag them up and deliver them to the paper mills in Thiviers.

'Piarrouty, you must pass by and collect our "scraps" as you call them. I'm sure we have some old rags we can give you. For free, of course,' Alain added.

'Thank you, Alain,' replied the ragman, doffing his large hat. 'I'll call by next week. You live on the Bretanges estate in Beaussac, don't you?'

'Yes. When you come, tell my parents I sent you.'

Alain noticed that the ragman, usually so cheerful, had a melancholy air about him. It seemed as though the heavy weighing hook he carried on his back was dragging him down.

'Is something bothering you, Piarrouty? Your son's not with you today. He's not ill, is he?' asked Alain.

Piarrouty shook his head and put his hat back on. On the horizon, beyond the shrivelled yellow grass and juniper bushes and well beyond the Nizonne marshes with their stagnant water that poisoned cattle and spread disease and epidemics, Alain noticed a small white trail of smoke from a steam train.

'Périgueux is sending whole trainloads of oats to feed the horses in Lorraine,' said Mazière, who was standing next to the rag collector.

Alain galloped along the curved path that led up the hill to Hautefaye and then pulled gently on the reins. His horse slowed down with a flick of his head. They came to a stop outside the school – an isolated building just beyond the main village. Alain jumped from the saddle, using a cork oak for support. He could tell it was a softwood tree from the feel of the bark.

'Here, Thibassou, put my horse with the others. I'm entrusting him to you,' he commanded, holding the reins out to a boy of fourteen and proffering a coin.

'Thank you, Monsieur de Monéys,' the boy said, delighted.

'Alain!' exclaimed a voluptuous woman who was sitting on a chair nearby, in the shade of a lime tree. She looked up briefly from her embroidery and met his gaze.

'How are you, Madame Lachaud? Where's your husband? Are you teaching even though it's the fair today?'

The schoolmaster's wife had soft round arms and wide hips, and the top buttons of her blouse were undone. She was in no hurry to do them up. On her left stood a young girl of twenty-three who was trying to recite the alphabet.

'Are you no longer ironing clothes in Angoulême, Anna?' asked Alain, surprised to see her in the village.

'I decided to come back. Do you remember me, Monsieur de Monéys?'

'Oh yes! I sent you a letter, but you never replied.'

'That's because I don't know how to write.'

'It must be two years and three months since I last saw you. You're even prettier than you were before.'

She blushed – a wild, dark-haired beauty. Thibassou seemed to share Alain's opinion and was undressing her with his eyes. Anna modestly lowered her gaze and started reciting her alphabet again:

'A, B, C, er . . .'

'Begin again, Mademoiselle Mondout,' commanded Madame Lachaud, watching Alain all the while. 'You'll get there because you're clever.'

The schoolmistress was kind and devoted, and possessed a fair amount of tact. They were interrupted by someone calling for Anna.

'What are you doing at school, at your age, and especially when we're so busy at the inn? Forget that and come and lend a hand. Later, you can take the goats to the mayor's barn so the ladies will have something to drink.'

'Yes, Uncle Élie.'

Anna Mondout left. Alain watched her go. Madame Lachaud sighed. Her breasts were covered in beads of sweat and she blew down her open blouse to keep herself cool.

'Even though we live in such a prosperous area, people are still illiterate. Only half of the town councillors know how to write their own names. Only nine boys in the whole area are at school.'

'What do you expect, Madame Lachaud? A child at school

16

is one less pair of hands at home or in the fields. Surely you understand that.'

He left the teacher's wife, who nodded in agreement and hitched up her skirt slightly.

'They have their troubles and their tears deserve my sympathy,' said Alain to himself. A pedlar by the roadside was taking the most marvellous trinkets out of his bags – gold rings, caricatures and magic mirrors for lovers. When someone breathed on the glass, the words 'I love you' would appear. The pedlar showed one to Alain, who exhaled and then stood back. On the glass, instead of his reflection, he could see a grey mist. When he looked closely, he could make out the letters of 'I love you'.

He continued onwards, limping slightly as though he had a piece of grit in his boot. He took a small fob watch from his waistcoat. It was two o'clock. In the village, the Saint-Roch fair was in full swing. He had arrived safely.

3

ARRIVAL IN HAUTEFAYE

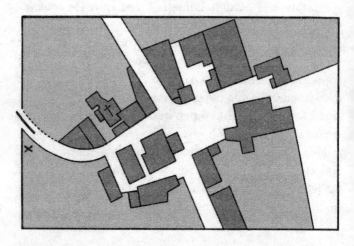

Alain was hailed on all sides as villagers jostled each other to let him through. The crowd divided, forming a semicircle. Seen from the sky, it looked like a smile. He entered and the human mouth closed behind him.

'The whole place is teeming!'

On his left, he could see the triangular garden between the priest's house and the church. The adjacent meadow had been transformed into a pig and donkey market for the day. He headed in that direction. The fair had not extended to the meadows on the right because they were blocked off by a low dry-stone wall.

People continued to flock up to Hautefaye from the surrounding countryside. They were dressed in their Sunday best – flat caps, smocks, clogs and ribbons. Each held a stick or cattle prod to chivvy along their livestock. Alain watched them wind their way in columns up to the top of the hill where the village sat, with it's magnificent view.

'What a lot of people have come for the Saint-Roch fair this year! Don't you agree, Antoine Léchelle?'

'Oh, good day, Monsieur de Monéys. Yes, I've never seen such a crowd. Twice as many people as usual. Six or seven hundred, they say, which is surprising in a village of just forty-five souls. The crowds stretch right to the other side of the village and the fair goes down to the dried-up lake.'

'I wouldn't be surprised if all the inhabitants of all the surrounding hamlets had decided to gather here today. Probably everyone within a fifteen-mile radius has turned up. How are you, Antoine?'

'Things were better when we had some water,' replied Antoine Léchelle, a wicker basket at his feet. 'Feuillade hasn't seen a drop these last eight months. The crops have all withered. They've shrivelled up in the heat wave. Our cattle are dying.' The worried villager toyed idly with his hat. 'Some people say it's a comet. I do hope it won't land on our heads! The barometer's still rising.'

Behind him, a couple of young calves struggled to keep their balance.

'You don't seem to have any females there, Antoine. I'm looking for a heifer for our Bertille.'

'They're with the other cows over there by the dried-up lake.'

'And how's business?'

'Bad. We just can't find any cattle dealers prepared to take the animals off our hands. I've never known anything like it. Everything is going wrong this year and the hens are barely laying either.'

'Put your eggs in the shade, Antoine. They'll bake in the sun.'

'Silly me! What's the matter with me today?'

Alain continued on his way, trying to beat a path through the horseflies that buzzed relentlessly around the livestock. He was surrounded by the stench of animals, the shouts of horse dealers and the low drone of conversation. From time to time he would overhear the odd snippet: 'This heat! Soon we'll be trying to get water from stones!' 'My throat's as dry as kindling. I'm almost afraid that if I spit, I'll start a fire!' A little old man who sold umbrellas was complaining he hadn't sold enough this year. He was speaking to Sarlat, a tailor from Nontronneau. Sarlat peered through his glasses at Alain as he passed, recognised the summer suit that he himself had made, gave Alain a thumbs up, winking to let him know that it looked good on him. The smell of frying meat and doughnuts hung in the air, but hardly anyone could afford to buy them. Someone was telling a story:

'So, the prefect of Ribérac went up to the mayor here in Hautefaye and asked, "Do you have any rebels in your region?" To which the mayor replied, "We've got brown bulls and black bulls, but no re-bulls!"'

'That Bernard Mathieu, he does come out with them. I don't know where he gets them from! He says such funny things,' chuckled a cobbler.

20

Despite the laughter around him, Alain had the impression that, this year, the place was pretending to be jolly. Sweating men tanned from the sun spread lard and rubbed garlic on their crusts of bread, which they swallowed down, rolling their worried eyes as they ate. On the other side of the road, Alain spotted the ragman he had overtaken on his horse earlier and to whom he had promised his 'scraps'. The man was sitting on the low dry-stone wall looking stricken.

'What's wrong with him this year?'

'Piarrouty learnt of his son's death yesterday,' explained a nearby man. 'He was shot in the head by a machine gun at Reichshoffen. A letter was sent to the mayor's house in Lussas. It was from one of the boy's injured friends who'd found him shot to smithereens. He'd even picked a lucky number, but a pharmacist's son who had an unlucky one bought it from him at Pons.'

The old ragman remained prostrate, his weighing hook across his thighs and a bottle of wine at his feet. He was distraught that he had sold his son to replace someone else. A loud droning sound came from the crowd. Small knots of people started to form. The heat was becoming heavy and oppressive.

Alain shook hands with the friendly villagers as he passed. Small landowners like himself, at the fair to do business, wandered amongst the crowd. The opulent glint of rings on their fingers made them easy to identify. They stopped to talk to tenant farmers about breaking the terms of their lease, and said they would discuss the matter again on St Michael's day, when it was the tradition for bosses and workers to settle their yearly accounts.

'Oh, Alain,' said Pierre Antony, a friend and neighbour, as he approached, 'I wanted to congratulate you on being elected unanimously as leader of Beaussac town council! There never was a worthier candidate.'

'Amédée must be so proud!' added a stonemason from Beaussac, referring to Alain's father. Then he asked, 'What's this plan of yours to divert the Nizonne that everyone's talking about?'

'Well, Jean Frédérique, it's a question of changing the river's course slightly. At the moment, a lot of water runs into the fields and is wasted. Uncultivated land will be transformed into pastureland and our insalubrious countryside will become hospitable and prosperous. People will benefit from these works for hundreds of years to come. I finished my report this morning and I shall send it to the government shortly.'

'Well, if you manage to convince those men in the ministry, then it won't be a waste of ink,' said Jean Frédérique, clasping Alain's hands warmly.

'You should stand for election to Parliament!' exclaimed Antony admiringly, flattering Alain.

'Oh, it is quite enough to be deputy mayor of Beaussac. My political ambition stops there,' he replied. He then asked the stonemason if he had spotted the carpenter from Fayemarteau in the crowd.

'Brut? I saw him earlier at one of the inns, but I can't remember whether it was Élie Mondout's or Mousnier's place.'

Alain glanced in the direction of the two inns in the centre of the village. They were packed. Men clustered around the tables and bottles were being passed around. There were so many people at the inns that Anna Mondout – the beautiful young girl who wanted to learn to read and write – was also bringing carafes of wine to the fair's entrance. She went over and served the horse traders, who were leaning against the priest's garden wall. They clinked their glasses, which flashed in the light.

'To the Emperor! To victory! To the destruction of Prussia and the death of Bismarck! If he ever dares to come to Hautefaye, we'll give him something to remember us by!'

Anna moved on to the labourers, gelders and wheelwrights, and filled their glasses with the nectar.

'Is this rainwater you're bringing us?'

'It's Noah, a white wine from Rossignol.'

'Blow me, that's strong!' said the men, tasting it and giving their verdict.

They paid their three sous, but thought that the wine was rather expensive. Anna – a sweet, pale girl with dark eyes and long eyelashes, wearing a grey and green dress – went on her way. Her straw hat blew off and her hair glinted red in the sun. Nearby, a pedlar was trying to sell a bundle of newspapers that had just arrived from Nontron. Even those who only knew how to read a few basic words in large print were snapping them up and trying to decipher the front page of the *Dordogne Echo*. Some of them were holding the paper upside down.

'I don't have my glasses. Can somebody read what it says?'

A broad-shouldered man in a black frock-coat read aloud the front-page headline above the five columns that

23

Alain had not wanted to read to his mother. 'DEFEAT AT FROESCHWILLER, REICHSHOFFEN, WOERTH AND FORBACH,' he announced, and then summed up the article below and gave his opinion. 'Things aren't going as well as hoped for the French armies at the border. The Emperor is done for. They're out of ammunition.'

Alain recognised the arrogant voice. It belonged to his cousin, Camille de Maillard.

'This pointless war, supposedly "fresh and joyous", is turning into a disaster,' he continued. 'Yet the Minister for War promised that "we are ready, more than ready. This will be a Sunday stroll from Paris to Berlin." Well, that's news to me, because Reichshoffen was a massacre.'

Piarrouty rose from his perch on the low, stone wall and turned to face the crowd. Around Alain's cousin, the news hit like a punch in the stomach.

'That's not true!' cried someone in protest. 'That's impossible! You don't know what's going on. To say that our emperor, who beat the Austrians in Italy and the Russians in the Crimea, isn't capable of holding back a few Prussians. Come now . . .'

'Our army has had to retreat to the Moselle!' responded de Maillard. 'It says so in the newspaper.'

Silence descended on the villagers who had gathered around de Maillard, the bearer of bad news. Many of them stared at their feet or gazed into the distance. The labourer from Javerlhac was sad that his glass was already empty and that he couldn't afford to refill it.

'You're an idiot,' he said.

'You're no more able to read than we are,' said a sawyer

from Vieux-Mareuil, examining a large fly crawling on his finger.

'The French will never retreat!' shouted a butcher from Charras, flicking the fly away as it came to land on his nose.

But de Maillard was emphatic. By saying that he knew for certain that the most recent battles had been even bloodier than reported in the *Dordogne Echo*, he was spreading panic amongst the relatives of soldiers. He said the government had ordered that the real numbers of dead be hushed up in case people started to worry. He said the war was lost, that Napoleon III was beaten and that perhaps nothing could stop the Prussians from taking over France.

'Regrettably,' he said, wincing, but nobody heard his sigh.

His pessimistic analysis of the situation caused indignation. A donkey brayed. Pigs banged their snouts against the fences. Two men in leather aprons carrying goads chivvied along a calf. The tinsmiths started to bang on their cauldrons with mallets. Horse traders, whips slung over their shoulders, moved closer, their voices growing louder. The strong wine was already going to people's heads.

'It's awful to hear such things. To think that some people are happy about what's happening!' grumbled a villager under his breath, fiddling with his shirt-tails and not daring to look up.

'Long live the militia!' shouted somebody, already tipsy on cheap wine.

Camille de Maillard's servant, Jean-Jean, who was standing nearby, must have sensed danger. Failed businesses, drought and now fear of invasion were poisoning the fair's atmosphere. He whispered urgently into his master's ear. As de Maillard turned his head sideways, Alain could not fail to recognise his sideburns, cut in the style of old King Louis-Philippe. Suddenly, the arrogant young man bolted, pushing people out of his way, and jumping over the low wall to the right of the road with Jean-Jean at his heels. They ran across the sloping field and headed for a small wood. Three villagers jumped the barrier as well and followed them. It was almost like a children's game, like watching little tin soldiers on a green baize surface. The farmers soon fell behind, their boots hampering their progress. De Maillard and his servant fled as quickly as they could. People seemed furious that they had managed to escape. Their pursuers returned, climbed back over the low, stone wall and surveyed the crowd.

'Now now, my friends, what's going on?' said Alain, limping towards them.

'It's your cousin,' explained a pedlar. 'He shouted, "Long live Prussia!"'

'What? No! Come now, I was standing just here, and that's not what I heard at all! And I know de Maillard well enough to be sure that he would never say such a thing. "Long live Prussia"? That's almost as ridiculous as shouting "Down with France!"'

'What did you just say?'

'I beg your pardon?'

'You said "Down with France!"'

'What? No, of course I didn't!'

'Yes, you did! You said "Down with France!"'

'But no, I didn't say that. I—'

'All those who heard him cry "Down with France!" raise your hand!' said the pedlar, addressing the people standing by the low wall.

'Oh, I heard him say "Down with France!"' said a voice, and a hand shot up.

Other fists were raised, five, then ten. Some villagers who may not even have heard the question saw hands go up and raised theirs too. People asked their neighbours what had happened.

'Someone said "Down with France!"'

A forest of hands went up to vouch for the fact.

'Who shouted "Down with France!"?'

'He did.'

Jean Campot appeared on Alain's left and twisted his ear. His brother Étienne let go of Jupiter's halter and dealt him a powerful blow. Jean Frédérique, coming up on his right, drove his mason's fist deep into Alain's stomach.

4

THE LOW DRY-STONE WALL

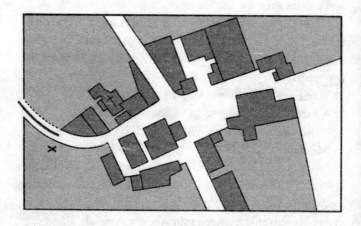

Alain knelt at the side of the road, gasping for breath. His eyes were closed and a grey mist descended. He waited for the words 'I love you' to come into focus, but instead heard shouts.

'Filth! Scoundrel!'

He opened his eyes, raised his head and saw dozens of angry faces surrounding him. Their eyes, which had previously held only kindness, now contained a venom which was terrible to see. Having regained his breath, Alain rose and spoke to them.

'You've misunderstood me, my friends,' he croaked. 'You're mistaken.'

'You were rejoicing in our enemies' success,' said one man, shaking his fist at Alain.

'I wasn't!'

'You're smiling!'

'No, I'm not!'

'You'd watch as they killed us all and spared your life!'

'No. In a week's time I'll be a simple soldier, fighting for France.'

'You're sending money to the Prussians!'

'Why would I send money to the enemy when I'm due to join the troops? That would be madness!'

Antony arrived and found Alain deathly pale. 'Get away from here quickly,' he urged in Alain's ear.

Alain turned to leave but could not escape. Some men had clambered over the dry-stone wall and stationed themselves behind it to stop him fleeing as his cousin had done. In any case, he would not have been able to run quickly or far with his limp. A wave of dizziness washed over him. Alain watched Piarrouty walk slowly towards him, clutching his weighing hook. Alain's legs felt like loose bundles of rags. He struggled to keep his balance, looking rather like one of Antoine Léchelle's newborn calves. Antoine Léchelle himself ripped off Alain's jacket spinning him round, then shouted abuse at him just like the other villagers.

'Muck! Scum!'

Alain felt as if he were living a nightmare. He cast around for a face that wasn't filled with hatred. Antony had been grabbed by the scruff of the neck and pushed to the back of the crowd, with shouts of 'Get out of here!' Never before had Alain seen such madness. The villagers were turning the whole thing into a violent farce.

'My dear, dear friends,' Alain said, trying in vain to restore peace. His pleas were met only with abuse. The villagers cared nothing for his achievements now. He was caught in an angry storm, a whirlwind of insults. What grim fortune for Alain, being trapped in such an appalling situation. He might as well have been a bear's plaything. Switches whipped viciously at his cheeks. He was hit with whips and riding crops - his clothes now looked as if they belonged to a court jester, and he had a button missing. The situation was getting out of hand. Where had that stain come from? Ah yes, from misfortune. With a thud, a cattle prod knocked his straw hat down over his eyes.

Shouts of 'Bravo! Good shot!' rang through the air. Alain wanted to put his hat back on properly but it was snatched from his hands and flew into the crowd. People passed it round, argued over it and tried it on. Behind them a ratter was grabbing vermin from a copper laundry tub teeming with the grey beasts, and killing them with his teeth. At his fairground stall, Old Moureau was offering people the chance to stone cockerels to death.

'Three goes, one sou. If you kill a cock, you keep it!' he called.

Leaning against the wall of the priest's garden, Anna Mondout looked over at Alain, shocked. Her arresting yet fragile gaze betrayed infinite goodness. Being of a sensitive nature, she could tell that Alain was close to tears. He was afraid. He needed rescuing fast and effectively at all costs. Thankfully, help was at hand. Philippe Dubois and Mazerat — a villager in overalls and a bearded woodcutter

— intervened. Skilfully, they managed to intercept blows aimed at Alain.

'Stop!' shouted Bouteaudon, a miller from Connezac, stepping in as well.

'He's a traitor, a spy, an enemy . . . a Prussian!' shouted Jean Frédérique, pointing at Alain. Antony, his face swollen, came back and squared up to him.

'He's a Prussian!' chorused everyone behind Jean Frédérique, and others even further behind, took up the cry, 'Come on! We've caught a Prussian!'

'A Pruuuu-ssiaaan!' yelled Jean Frédérique at the top of his voice.

'You imbecile!' spluttered Antony. 'He's no Prussian, he's Alain de Monéys! I heard you asking him to explain his plans to divert the Nizonne just ten minutes before you kicked him in the stomach. You were talking to him!'

'I've never talked to a Prussian!'

'Dear God, Jean Frédérique, you even voted for him!'

'That's not true!'

'I saw you, last Wednesday, coming out of the polling booth in Beaussac town hall.'

'I didn't vote for him!'

'But, Frédérique, it was unanimous. Everybody voted for Alain.'

'I did *not* vote for him!'

'Quite right too!' clamoured voices from nearby. 'We don't vote for Prussians!'

'Jean Frédérique, hey, wake up, Frédérique!' exclaimed Antony, waving his arms about as though trying to rouse his companion from a dream. But the Beaussac stonemason managed to reach round Antony and whack Alain full in the face with a stick, causing him to cry out in pain.

'Argh! Oh!'

'Did you hear that? He said "*Ach so*". He speaks German! He's a Prussian!'

Men in wooden clogs – boys and old men, but very few in between, since they were all at war – clamoured:

'He's a Prussian! Pru-ssi-an, ru-ffi -an, Pru-ssi-an!'

Alain had never had a nickname before, but it seemed that this one was sticking. In vain he repeated, 'I am Alain de Monéys, Alain de Monéys,' but his words fell on deaf ears. People refused to accept his true identity. Despite the crowd's obstinacy, Bouteaudon, Dubois, Mazerat and Antony continued to proclaim Alain's innocence, but the mob just would not listen.

'He's our enemy and he must pay for it!' said a voice from the sea of straw hats bobbing in front of them.

An ill-tempered man barely known to Alain shouted that Alain was a Prussian and raised his bludgeon. Mazerat blocked his arm.

'For heaven's sake, you're about to hit Alain de Monéys!'

'Shut up and let us defend our country. He's a Prussian. Jesus Christ, let's get him!'

Someone kicked Alain in the buttocks.

'Come on then, dirty Prussian, let's hear you shout "Long live the Emperor!" Shout it, shit bag, shout it.'

'Long live the Emperor!' Alain proclaimed.

'Louder, Prussian, louder!'

Alain was hit with enough force to kill a donkey. People stabbed his arms and shoulders repeatedly with goads. His shirt tore.

'Hit him hard enough and maybe the rain will come!'

People jostled to get to the front. Alain recoiled from their attack, backing up against the dry-stone wall. Suddenly, he received such a sharp blow to the skull that he thought his head would explode. He turned and saw his absurd shadow sliding down the wall on which Piarrouty was standing, holding a hook covered in blood. Alain reeled from the attack. He could hear cheers and the thunder of loose stones as the dry-stone wall collapsed from where he lay right up to the cherry tree further along. He got up quickly, slipping and sliding comically on the rubble, cradling his head one minute and then flinging his arms out in front of him the next. The sleeves of his yellow nankeen suit were splattered with red.

'Oh no, my suit is stained. I can't go back to Bretanges like this. What will I tell my mother?'

He felt a surge of deep shame. He had a gash on his head and blood was running down his neck. Tears were running down his face too, though not many. Things would be resolved; people would see reason eventually. In the background, Anna stood terrified, her hands over her mouth, watching with the beautiful dark eyes that had captured his heart. But Alain was dragged under by another hail of blows.

The poor unlucky soul had fallen victim to a horde of phantoms who danced wildly in the scorching summer heat. Antony found himself pushed to the back of the crowd once more, along with Alain's other supporters. Alain was alone. Mazière – the man who had been talking to Piarrouty when he had overtaken them on his way to the village – was shouting shrilly. It was giving Alain a headache. All those faces, smells and shouts!

A harsh, harpy-like cry rose up and Alain turned in the direction it came from. It was the schoolteacher's wife. The schoolteacher's wife? She was standing on a small cart, its shafts pointing upwards.

'Hang the Prussian!' screeched Madame Lachaud, puffing out her chest, her breasts bursting out of her blouse. Almost immediately, a chant of 'Hang him!' broke out and rippled through the air, like the national flag.

'Hang me?' echoed Alain incredulously.

5

THE OLD CHERRY TREE

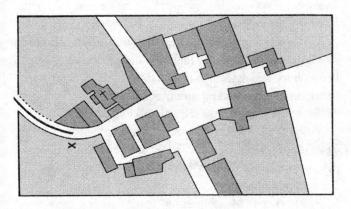

Étienne Campot deftly released the hemp halter that was fastened round Jupiter's thick neck and held it out to his younger brother.

'Here, take this to hang the Prussian from that old cherry tree opposite the priest's garden.' He turned to Thibassou and ordered, 'Thibassou, you're quick and agile, go and help Jean.'

And so amid shouts of 'Prussian bastard!' Alain was seized and bound. Thibassou, the very boy Alain had paid to look after his horse, scaled the old cherry tree as nimbly as a squirrel.

The gnarled trunk of the centuries-old tree was S-shaped and a long, thick branch overhung the collapsed wall.

Thibassou was thrilled that this execution would give him the chance to do a man's job, and set to work with zeal. He attached a rope to the branch while Jean Campot fashioned a noose around Alain's neck. He then clambered higher and balanced on a branch, looking out at the crowd.

'Anna Mondout, Anna! Look, I'm helping hang the Prussian!' he called.

Thibassou bounced up and down to test the tree's strength, but the branch snapped, falling on several people below and taking him with it. The injured men swore furiously at Alain and hit him in retaliation.

'Bloody Prussian, you're really pissing us off!'

At the foot of the tree, tempers were fraying and a fight broke out between farmers and pit sawyers. Roumaillac – a man who sold planks in Vieux-Mareuil – was yelling at the elder Campot brother.

'What a stupid idea to hang a Prussian from a cherry tree! Everyone knows their branches break easily. You should know that, Étienne. Call yourself a farmer?'

'Yes, but ... but ...' stammered the elder Campot brother. 'For goodness' sake, Roumaillac, we're not used to doing things like this. Personally, I've never hanged a Prussian before. I don't even know how it's done!'

From under the tree, Alain reminded them of one small detail. 'I'm not Prussian. My friends, you're about to kill a French soldier.'

Étienne Campot hit him for the second time.

'Quiet, Bismarck!'

'That's who we really should be hanging!' applauded the crowd.

'How about if we pulled the rope higher, draped it over a branch and tied it to the trunk?' came a voice from the mob.

'Not a bad idea,' said Roumaillac, suddenly the expert. 'It'll be stronger. To work, men!'

Alain was gasping for breath. He could hear a voice calling and see two hands waving from the back of the crowd.

'Father! Father! Father Saint-Pasteur!' called Anna. She vaulted the gate into the priest's garden and ran to bang on the door of the house.

'What is it?' asked a voice as the door opened.

'Th-th-they're over there in the road. At least a hundred of them. They've surrounded Monsieur de Monéys and they're beating him, beating him like a carpet! They want to hang him. They're going to hang him, I tell you!' said Anna, gasping as Alain had earlier.

The priest went back inside and returned immediately, holding a big gun.

'You have a weapon?' asked Anna, shocked.

'An heirloom from my uncle. He was in the military.'

The local priest, still in his cassock, jumped over his garden wall into the road.

'Let me through! Make way!' He pointed his gun at anyone who blocked his path. 'Let me through!'

'Leave him to us, Father. He's only getting what he deserves. He's a Prussian!'

'Shut up. You are blaspheming, you idiots. He's your neighbour!'

'He was the one blaspheming. He shouted "Down with France!"'

'Get back, get back, you fools,' boomed the priest, in his strong Pyrenees accent. He was an athletic man, with broad shoulders and a thick neck. He approached Alain and pointed his weapon at the old ragman, who was once more raising his hook above Alain's battered head.

'Put down that hook, Piarrouty, or I'll shoot!' shouted the priest, holding his gun to Piarrouty's face.

'But, Father, my son was shot to smithereens because of him.'

'Put it down or I'll shoot!'

Antony went over to the priest, grabbed the ragman's tool, flung it aside and loosened the rope round Alain's neck.

'Father, you and Antony are traitors!' voices cried, growing louder and louder as Antony untied Alain.

'Shout "Down with France!" now, if you're brave enough,' someone called out.

'No, sir, I shout "Long live France!"' boomed the priest in his pious voice, turning round. 'I take collections for our injured and offer up prayers for our fighters. You'd know that if you came to church more often.'

'Right, well, if you truly do say "Long live France!" then you should pay for our drinks,' demanded a builder from Javerlhac. 'Give us the communion wine for free. Then we'll be able to drink to the health of the Emperor!'

The priest faltered for a second and then said, 'With pleasure. I'll wait for you at my house. And Monsieur de Monéys shall join us for a drink.'

'Who?'

'The man you've been attacking, you miscreants!'

'The Prussian?'

Several people abandoned their prey and rushed over to the priest's garden. He handed out glasses and personally poured wine for everybody present. Anna filled goblets as well, much to the indignation of her uncle, who happened to be passing by.

'I can't believe what I'm seeing. Rather than lending us a hand at the inn, you choose to help the priest, who's stealing our customers?'

'But, Uncle Élie, it's because . . . If you knew . . . if you knew what . . .'

'No, I don't want to know! Get yourself back to our place, fetch the milking pails and take the goats to the mayor's goat shed. The ladies are waiting.'

'But Uncle . . .'

'Now! Or do you want to go back to your ironing job in Angoulême?' he ordered, dragging his niece away.

Meanwhile, people were happily quaffing the communion wine.

'Ah, this wine warms your insides.'

'Yes, it's a good thing we showed that Prussian what for, or we wouldn't have had anything to drink!'

The priest refilled their glasses and drank to their health, hoping to put an end to the violence with his gesture of hospitality. He welcomed them as he welcomed them into his church each week. Jesus forgives a multitude of sins through the words of a priest.

'Drink as much as you like but, for heaven's sake, don't waste your breath hitting an innocent man so hard!'

Standing close to Alain, Thibassou hesitated for a moment and then shouted, 'Well, I'm a man now, I almost hanged a Prussian!'

'To the health of the Empress and the young imperial Prince!' clamoured family men, inspired by the youth's words.

The wind whipped around the priest's garden, which soon became crowded. People who had been lingering by the cherry tree eventually left to make the most of the free wine as well. 'The priest told us to; we do everything the priest tells us!' Some people headed to the donkey market or to the various inns to show off their sticks covered in Alain's blood. Others started trading by the roadside again: 'So, how much did you want for those scrawny little hens?' The crowd broke up and relaxed.

The big fallen cherry branch creaked and its dry leaves rustled in the breeze. Shoes and boots crunched over the heap of stones from the broken wall. Antony, Dubois and Mazerat had returned and were supporting Alain under his arms.

'Where shall we take him? We can't make him cross the meadow to the small wood. He would easily be spotted from the priest's garden and he can barely run,' said Dubois.

'And it would be risky to take him back to his horse,' replied Mazerat. 'A lot of his attackers have gone to boast of their deeds at the pig market. If they see him go by . . .'

'Why don't we take him to the town hall?' suggested Bouteaudon, who had just joined them.

'There isn't one in Hautefaye,' replied Antony. 'But we could take him to our mayor, the blacksmith. Come on, Alain, we'll go to Bernard Mathieu. We'll get you out of this mess. These men have lost their minds.'

'Thank you, Pierre; thank you, Philippe,' said Alain,

to Antony and Dubois. 'Thank you, my dear friends. If it hadn't been for you and the priest, I think they'd have torn me to shreds.'

Bouteaudon, the strong miller from Connezac, sat Alain on his forearms as if he were a sack of flour.

'Let me carry you, Monsieur de Monéys.'

'Oh, gladly, my friend,' said Alain, with a look of gratitude for the protector he had previously met only in passing.

'Why are you taking advantage of the priest's diversion to take him to the mayor?' called the Charras butcher angrily, following them.

'If there are any explanations to be had, they will take place before the Emperor's sole representative in this village,' replied Antony.

'Oh no, they won't! Leave him! He's ours!' exclaimed the butcher. 'I'm going to tell the others. Hey, men!'

Antony ignored his threats and asked Alain how he was feeling.

'My head really hurts.'

'That's not surprising. Piarrouty cracked your skull. But the mayor will send for Dr Roby-Pavillon from Nontron, he'll patch you up. You'll laugh about this later.'

'They thought I was a Prussian,' groaned Alain, his head throbbing, as they made their way through the village.

'That's because they refuse to see the truth. They're trying to get their own back for a defeat that they can't acknowledge,' said Dubois philosophically.

'By attacking you, these people believed that they were helping save the Emperor and France.'

'That's right.'

From that point, Alain floated along, dazed and staggering as if drunk. They had arrived.

6

THE MAYOR'S DOOR

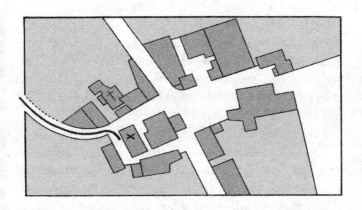

Having dared to think that the worst was over and everything would turn out fine, Alain began to realise that nothing was further from the truth.

'Hold your horses! You can't do that!' exclaimed a cheese-maker from Jonzac.

'He's the reason for our misfortune!' clamoured the crowd, giving voice to the cheese-maker's unspoken accusation.

Angry men flocked over from the priest's garden, the donkey and pig markets, and the inns at the centre of the village. Rioters were spreading the news.

'We found a Prussian at the fair!'

'A Prussian?'

Suddenly, insults rained down on Alain from all sides like a violent thunderstorm. He was afraid – this was not the roar of acclaim. They launched into a furious fresh attack, like an army. The men wore smocks and hats; the women had chignons, coarse skirts, and scarves on their heads.

'Hurry, hurry! Get the Prussian! Get the Prussian!'

At the side of the road, people were stealing from the priest's wood pile in order to arm themselves with 'stout sticks'. At least three hundred people had gathered, all with sticks, scythes and pitchforks. Once again, Alain was showered with blows. Bouteaudon, the Connezac miller, had his arms protectively round Alain. People hit him too and eventually he was forced to lay Alain on the ground.

The villagers' previous love and affection had turned to hate. Kneeling, Alain almost laughed to himself between the blows and his tears. It was as though earlier they had eased off the pressure for a moment, and granted his protectors some time, all the better to savour this renewed attack. Chaos reigned and there was a lust for blood.

'We don't want a Judas in Hautefaye! He must be killed!'

The net of hostile rumours was closing in. It was easy to believe this was a game at the funfair – knocking down skittles, climbing the greasy pole, a carousel ride, a sack race, or a more modern velocipede race. Old Moureau left his cockerel-stoning stall and kicked Alain so violently in the head that he dislodged a clump of hair. He rejoined the others and showed them the tip of his bloodied shoe, covered in hair.

'Bull's eye.'

'Bravo, you've won a cockerel!' shouted the villagers.

'You stupid old fool. You'd do better to think of the day when you'll have to account for yourself!' shouted Dubois, outraged, pointing his finger at the old man.

'Think what you will, good people, but things are not what they seem. I'm not a Prussian . . .' Alain reminded them in vain, struggling to sit up and protect his head. He was at the centre of a comedy of errors. Public condemnation wounded him with the prongs of pitchforks. What a regrettable state of affairs! Even fourteen-year-old Thibassou derived a perverse pleasure from hitting him, and he asked around for a big knife.

Alain's protectors struggled to help him over the few yards that now separated them from the narrow alley where the mayor's residence stood, opposite his smithy. The goat shed was just ahead.

'Bernard Mathieu! Bernard Mathieu!'

Three steps led up to the door of the house, which served as the town hall on council evenings and election days. The door opened and a burly man in his sixties emerged, chewing and wiping his hands on his tricolour sash, tied round his chest much like a napkin. He paused and observed Antony and Dubois with a frown as they brought Alain towards him.

'Your Worship, Your Worship! Look how people are attacking Monsieur de Monéys! We must protect him! Let him in!'

Suddenly the crowd surged into the lane, with hundreds of people clamouring to assault Alain amid a torrent of abuse. Faced with their caterwauling and whistling, Bernard Mathieu hurriedly turned and went back up the steps.

Mazerat lost patience with the mayor's dithering.

'Mayor, do something quickly! These men are mad! You know Monsieur de Monéys!'

'I know him, I know him . . . He's not from the village.'

Alain tried to protect himself with his forearms but, standing there forlornly in his tattered clothes, he did not have the strength.

'But, Bernard Mathieu, you must help us save him. What will happen if you don't?'

'What do you expect me to do with no police back-up? Who are these folks attacking him? Outsiders?' stuttered the mayor.

'You know them all! Look, there's Campot, Léchelle, Frédérique and everyone else. Order them to leave Alain alone.'

'Hey! You there! It's over. Do you hear me? Leave this man alone. If he needs punishing, call in the law,' said Bernard Mathieu, descending two steps.

'We are the law!' shouted Roumaillac.

'A law of fools!' commented Antony.

'Your Worship, I implore you, let him in!' begged Mazerat.

But the mayor's wife at the open window by the front door refused.

'So that they can come and smash our crockery? Whatever next? Bernard, come back and finish your dinner!' she commanded, resting her hands on the shoulders of her eight-year-old granddaughter, who was sobbing in panic at the sight of the fists and sticks raining down on Alain in a swirl of light, dust and mist.

'Alain, go and play somewhere else; you're making my little granddaughter cry,' requested the mayor, ever the attentive grandfather.

'I don't believe it. The mayor . . . This is outrageous,' said Bouteaudon, devastated.

'What are you going to do, Bernard?' asked Antony.

'Finish my supper.'

Alain looked over at the dwelling he was not allowed to enter. Behind the mayor, he could make out one bed, a broken sideboard and four chairs. The curtains at the window had once been white but were now spattered with squashed bugs. Hautefaye's mayor closed the door on the ugly, faded decor. A key turned twice in the lock. The mayor's moustachioed nephew, Georges, who was a baker in Beaussac, banged on the shutters that his aunt had just closed.

'Aunt! Uncle! Open up, if only for Monsieur de Monéys! We must protect him!'

'It's none of our business!'

Driven back against the wall, Alain appealed softly to the brutes.

'My friends, you're mistaken. I'm ready to suffer for France . . .'

'You'll suffer all right; we'll make sure you suffer!' said François Chambort, a blacksmith from Pouvrières, grabbing Alain by the hair. As children, they had fished for crayfish together. Alain was hurt to see his former playmate hatching some grisly plan right in front of his eyes, something vicious and relentless. François blew noisily on his hat and commanded in a cattle drover's voice, 'Take the Prussian

47

over the road to the smithy! I know what we can do! We can tie him to the frame and shoe him like a horse!'

7

THE BLACKSMITH'S FORGE

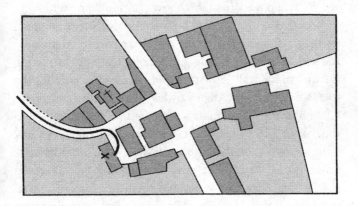

The Campot brothers dragged Alain to the smithy. Buisson and Mazière kicked him in the shins to hurry him along. Chambort was shouting out orders. The crowd surged forward.

'Castrate him while you're at it, the son of a bitch. Then he won't defile our women,' bayed Madame Lachaud.

They successfully manoeuvred Alain between the four posts of the frame used to restrain horses. Lying on his back between the wooden bars, his hands and feet bound, Alain shouted feebly, 'Long live the Emperor!' Men surrounded him, pressing in. The ordeal was endless. Straps and ropes were tightened, constricting his chest and throat. He choked. He struggled, his legs flailing wildly. Duroulet, a labourer from Javerlhac, pulled off Alain's brown boots and another man removed his purple silk socks. In the crowd, Lamongie – a stocky farmer with ginger hair – was brandishing a huge pair of pliers. Alain had known him as a boy; they had raided magpies' nests together.

'We'll clip the Prussian's hooves for him!' he said.

A puffed-up turkey fled between people's legs, flapping its wings. Lamongie gripped the lower part of Alain's big toe with his pincers and pulled as though he were extracting a nail from a wall. He staggered backwards, holding the toe in his pincers. Alain howled. The crowd sniggered. Chambort took Lamongie's place and held a horseshoe to the sole of Alain's lame foot. Suddenly, he banged in a nail with a single stroke, shattering his heel. The other twenty-six bones in Alain's foot seemed to splinter too. The pain rose to his knee, his groin and then tore into his chest, suffocating him. His shoulders tensed and he thought his head would explode. Chambort nailed a second shoe to the other foot. Alain's head jerked backwards, his eyes rolling. Memories surged into his mind. He felt like a ship being stormed by pirates shouting, 'Dirty beast!'

His body was weak and weary and his heels throbbed. The noise was deafening. His flesh was turning a ghastly colour. Alain was living a nightmare. The behaviour of his fellow creatures plunged him into despair. Earlier, on his way to the fair and unaware of the horrific fate that awaited him, he had been lost in the most wonderful reverie. Now, even the devil would have cried for mercy on seeing several of Alain's toes fly from Lamongie's pliers and hurtle through the air.

The schoolmaster's wife was pulling faces at the window, sticking out her tongue and slobbering on the grimy glass.

'Hurry!' shouted a voice. 'Hurry, drinks are on the priest! We've finished off the cheap communion wine, so now he's bringing vintage bottles up from the cellar. Everyone's invited!'

'First I must finish clipping the Prussian's hooves,' said Lamongie.

'We'll come back! Come and have a drink. Let him suffer. He won't go far trussed up like that. Volunteers can keep watch by the door while we wet our whistles. The priest has even opened his house and the church to hold more people. Come sit on the altar and get sozzled!'

The crowd went off, leaving Alain. He heard the door creak behind them. Five men, who must have crept around the outside of the smithy, stole into the room. There they found Alain covered in blood, still tied up, with horseshoes on his feet. He had no toes on his right foot. He was sure they would no longer want him in the army now, even on the Lorraine front. The men who had been keeping watch left to get drunk with the others.

Mazerat and the mayor's nephew made the most of the guards' absence. 'Quick, let's free him. Those fools haven't tied him up properly.'

Mazerat opened a penknife and sawed at the knots. Distraught, Antony propped Alain up and supported his bleeding head, cradling him and trying to comfort him, as far as it is possible to comfort a man in such a predicament.

'Hold firm, Alain! We'll get you out of here.'

'Is that you, Pierre?'

'Yes, it's me. They're monsters. They should be locked up.'

'They know not what they do.'

Bouteaudon crouched down and cupped Alain's face in his gentle miller's hands. Miraculously, Alain seemed to be smiling. Dubois took out a handkerchief and dabbed at Alain's brow, which was covered in sweat and dust. He even wiped the dried blood from Alain's eyes, so that he could open them again. Alain was finding it difficult to catch his breath, but the presence of his solicitous friends gave him new hope.

'We must tell my mother that I'll be back later than expected . . .'

Antony looked at him sadly. He was a good, simple man and a loyal friend, and it pained him to see Alain being treated this way. Suddenly young Thibassou burst into the smithy. He grabbed a large knife from the workbench and ran off towards the church, shouting, 'Quick! Quick! They've freed the Prussian!'

Mazerat and Bouteaudon slipped their heads under Alain's armpits to support him.

'That little bastard! Where can we take Monsieur de Monéys?' they groaned.

'To Mousnier's place,' suggested Antony. 'When he had to do some work on the inn, Alain lent him the money he needed interest free. He'll take him in.'

But they had barely left the smithy, heading for the town centre, when the mob arrived from the vicarage and barred their path.

'Leave him to us!' they shouted.

'This is Alain de Monéys!' Dubois reminded them. 'He has never wronged anyone! He's the only man in these parts who'll let you gather wood in his forests if you're short for the winter! And you can run after hares in his meadows without him setting his dogs on you!'

'Shut up, idiot!' bellowed Antoine Léchelle, grabbing Dubois by his shirt.

'Cut off his balls!' shrieked Madame Lachaud. Arms knocked Alain to his knees just below the mayor's window, which opened. The son of the Fayemarteau roofer, whom Alain had wanted to hire, whacked him in the face with a stick.

'Roland! You've just hit your father's friend!' exclaimed Antony.

'My father has no Prussian friends! Oh, look, here he is. Tell them, Father!'

His father, drunk on holy wine, raised his iron bar. Alain looked at him and said, 'Pierre Brut, it's me, I was hoping you would fix a barn roof . . .' But the roofer was deaf and blind to his pleas and hit him with all his strength. Others lashed his back and legs. With horseshoes on his feet and several toes missing, he stumbled and collapsed under the hail of metal blows.

'See the Prussian dance!' jeered the mob.

The mayor's nephew once again implored his uncle to give Alain shelter. From the window, Bernard Mathieu pointed to the sheep barn at the end of the lane.

'Put him in there. He'll be just as comfortable there as in my house until you can take him back to Bretanges.'

8

THE SHEEP BARN

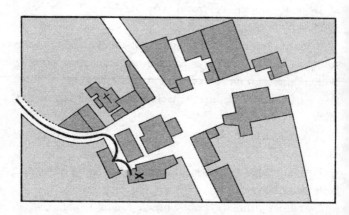

Mazerat the woodcutter and Bouteaudon the miller guarded the entrance to the tiny barn where they had taken Alain, for want of a better option. The mayor's nephew, the baker, stood with them, pitchfork in hand. Inside it was dimly lit, and Alain was lying on a pile of straw, which reeked of sheep's urine. A solitary ray of light slipped under the door, illuminating the barn and the hooves of three rams and a ewe, which all stood staring at Alain.

His appearance was grotesque. His tortured body burnt with pain. Breathing had become mechanical. The outlook was bleak. Feverishly, Alain muttered meaningless words, softly repeating his mother's name. The villagers continued to clamour outside. It is surprising how quickly people can lose their heads. Alain lay panting on the floor. With the three men barring the door and Antony and Dubois at his side, he started to think he might still get away alive.

'We'll do all we can to save you,' said Antony, reassuring him. 'But it's not easy with a cowardly mayor and faced with these madmen.'

'Thank you, thank you . . .'

Antony's patient words and actions were worthy of a saint.

'Oh, Monsieur de Monéys, those men!' gasped Dubois, as he turned Alain's face gently towards him.

'I look a fright, don't I?'

Dubois placed a ripe fig on Alain's lips and he sucked on it gingerly. Outside, the mob chanted, 'Pruss-ian! Pruss-ian!' It was becoming increasingly difficult for Mazerat and his men to block the entrance. Antony and Dubois decided to help them and slipped out, closing the door behind them.

'Have you all gone mad? When did you ever see a Prussian in Hautefaye?!' they yelled.

'He wanted to go to war despite being exempted!' shouted Bouteaudon. 'You all proclaim "Long live France!" but how many of you would do the same? Leave him alone and go and fight the Prussians where they really are – in Lorraine! That would be much braver than here at the fair where you're five hundred against your one neighbour!'

'Shut him up!' shrieked Mazière. 'Bring out the Prussian!'

Roumaillac and a handful of cronies had clambered onto the barn roof, pulled off some tiles and were relieving themselves! Piarrouty was shitting on Alain from above and hurling abuse. Alain was the victim of these people's inner monster, visible in their contorted faces. He lay there his heart close to breaking, as they pissed and shat on him. Thankfully his few defenders – like gentle lights in the mist – were protecting him, despite his gruesome appearance. Alain recognised Bernard Mathieu's voice yelling at the vile men on the roof.

'You're vandalising my building. Get down!' he shouted, probably from his window.

'We're still having a crap.'

'This is appalling! We're surrounded by cowards!' wailed Antony.

Chambort wanted to set fire to the barn. Someone dropped through the hole in the roof and landed in the straw. It was Thibassou, wielding the large knife he had taken from the blacksmith's workbench earlier. Idly tossing the handle from one hand to the other, he seemed to be mulling over particularly evil thoughts.

'I'm going to kill you,' he said. A pool of light shone on the straw nearby.

'But what have I done to you, Thibassou?' asked Alain anxiously. There was a wild, feral look in the boy's eyes.

Thibassou did not reply but shot Alain a look of disdain as he edged closer. The knife blade gleamed.

'Psst!' came a voice from behind them.

Anna was hidden in the dark at the back of the barn, close to two goats. Alain hadn't noticed her. The light coming in through the damaged roof made Anna stand out like a shining beacon sent to save him from despair. She hitched up her dress and called to Thibassou again: 'Psst!'

The boy was in a quandary. He was torn between

stabbing Alain and going to Anna. She raised her grey and green dress further. She perched on the edge of the feeding trough. Alain could see the smooth, silky skin of her calves and inner thighs and stored it in his memory. She was all sweetness, virtue and light. He was sure her bare flesh would smell fragrant and fresh. Her soft pubic hair rippled gently, clear as day, with an inviting innocence. She sat on the trough with her legs apart, her labia laughing like a clown's grin. The paleness of her belly could only have been stolen from the moon. It drove the boy wild. Desire swelled in his breeches like a mushroom in a field. Anna removed her dress, and, unable to resist the lure of her small breasts, the youth was compelled to rush forward and kiss them. Thibassou flew, lunged, letting his knife drop as he grabbed her. Her hands roamed over his body. The young devil seemed well practised. He was like a wily wolf, his body and mouth suddenly madly infatuated with her. The way he went at it! Anna turned to look at Alain. She did not lower her gaze. Her delightful breasts, under her tumbling dark hair, were living fruit savoured by lips intoxicated by their good fortune. Her lovely thighs, pert breasts, her back and stomach were a feast for the eyes and the hands. And the charming girl started to enjoy it. Thibassou drove a burning fire into her veins which sent her rump, hips and flanks wild. Beneath his shirt, his thrusting groin was untiring, inexhaustible, and he muttered, 'Oh, the bitch! What a little whore!' It was such a sexual frenzy that his entire body was lusting for more. The boy grabbed Anna's thighs and staggered forwards in the straw, knocking over a pail of milk. Clearly he was not afraid to go deep inside her.

Driven by heat and passion, covered with heavy beads of sweat, he made the most of his chance to take a local beauty. She writhed and arched and the scent she exuded drove him crazy. The air was awash with their sweat and panting. She was giddy and glowing with pleasure, all the while trying to keep her eyes on Alain. Her whole being – legs, hands, feet, heart – was ecstatic.

'Ahhhh!' Anna's voice was hoarse as she started to moan, while the riot continued on the other side of the door.

'Listen to him suffer! You've already done enough to him,' said Antony and Dubois, asking people to listen to the low moans emerging from the barn.

But it was Anna climaxing, all in an effort to distract the youth.

'Stay, stay, go on, do it again,' she said, whispering in his ear. To stop him attacking Alain, she moaned, 'More!'

'More, more!' came the cries of his attackers, thinking the plea came from Alain.

More? What a misunderstanding!

9

THE MAIN STREET

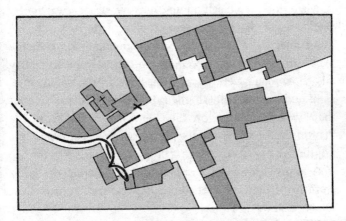

The door burst open. Men grabbed Alain by his shod feet and threw him into the muck heap.

'You want more? We'll give you more!'

Nobody noticed Thibassou, dragged by Anna to the feeding trough. Alain overheard his protectors whispering nearby.

'How can we get them to leave the alley long enough for us to help him escape?'

Dubois had an idea and elbowed his way through the crowd to Alain.

'Wouldn't you rather be shot than beaten even more?' he asked, crouching down.

'Oh yes, let them shoot me . . .'

'Do you hear that, everyone? Go and get your guns! Quick, go home and fetch your guns!' said Dubois, straightening up.

'No, no guns!' sang Mazière and the others. 'He must suffer.'

Alain found himself in the narrow street once more. He knew the place but it was no comfort to him now. He was subjected to ever more violent threats and gruesome propositions. He also received more deadly blows. They all – how many were there? – blackened his name further, calling him a coward. Oh, the irony! Everyone was venting their worst excessess on him. The flag flying from the mayor's house witnessed the horror with disgust. Alain was not the only person deserving of pity.

A man with glasses and beady eyes – Sarlat, the tailor from Nontronneau – yelled at Alain and tore at his yellow nankeen suit.

'Filthy Prussian!'

'Why do you say that? You know him. You dressed him! And now you're ripping clothes that you made!' yelled Antony.

'I did not make this suit!'

'Strewth!' exploded Antony. 'Look, there, in the lining, that's your label sewn in there. Your name is on it, Sarlat!'

'Oh, the filthy Prussian!' exclaimed the tailor, yanking off a sleeve. 'He's been stealing our clothes as well!'

They clawed at his suit and his shirt. Bare-chested, Alain was at the mercy of the rabble. They dragged him to the end of the street. Alain could see the open door of the church opposite. A flaking crucifix hung behind the altar. Christ's hair looked too long and it seemed as if he had only been put there so he could gaze down wrathfully at the barbarians.

The priest continued to drink to the Emperor in order to distract as many of the angry mob as possible. But people had been praying for a while for a miracle to happen and had seen no results. So he was now less sure of success. Alain fell to his knees in front of the church, which had become a tavern where the wine would eventually run out.

'Tell them that if they let me go, I'll pay for drinks as well. Crack open a barrel,' he begged. Mazerat was appalled.

'We won't drink wine from a Prussian!' shouted one of his persecutors, who had overheard.

'Oh, my friends, my friends . . .'

'Are you still talking?' asked a man, surprised. 'Here!' He smashed an iron bar down on Alain's mouth. Alain choked and spat out blood and broken teeth.

The church clock struck three. Alain heard the bells chime, tolling out his pain. He was seized by the mob, who raised him above their heads and engulfed him. The procession set off up the town's main street. Alain lay flat on his back under the mocking sun, gasping for breath. He felt like a carnival statue, rather like the Black Virgin of Rocamadour or St Léonard of Limousin. Insults continued to rain down on him and the pain in his head was unbearable. He howled as he was passed from person to person. He felt something inside him die, destroyed by the mob's madness.

Head lolling back, Alain was surprised to see the upside-down faces of his helpless protectors. He had thought he would never see them again, certainly not on the way to his grisley end! The whole affair was tragic. No one but the devil would delight in such a vicious game. Lord have pity on those men. They flung him to the ground. Alain glimpsed whips, batons and hooks in their hands, and felt the thwack of sticks.

'Knock him out! Knock him out!'

People jostled to get at him, vying to deal the hardest blow. Thibaud Devras, a pig merchant from Lussac, raised his stick and waited for Alain to leave his head exposed. Alain had paid for his daughter's headstone. He tried to remind Devras of this as he hit him full in the face.

The crowd pushed and shoved in their attempts to strike him and leave their mark on the enemy. One man hit him and then stepped back, leaving his place to another, who, once he had struck Alain, stood aside to be quickly replaced by someone else. The instinctive, collective nature of the massacre diluted responsibility. The bloodshed gave youngsters at the fair the opportunity to prove themselves and join the men. Thibassou was back again. The fourteen-year-old swaggered up and down the streets of Hautefaye, showing off his bloodstained baton. He vaunted his ferocity.

'Hey, you, have you hit him? No? You're a coward!' he said, as he and Pierre Brut's son questioned a boy of their own age.

'Go and give him what for, 'Poleon,' a mother commanded her five-year-old.

The child hit Alain. He withdrew his hand and it was spattered with blood. Old Moureau urged people to throw stones at Alain's head.

'Three goes, one sou. If you kill the Prussian, you take him home.' He handed out stones, turning the killing into a sideshow. People trod on Alain with their left foot, superstitiously believing it would bring them luck. They thrashed him as if they were threshing wheat.

'We haven't threshed much wheat thanks to you, scum! *Lébérou!*'

Alain was being likened to the mythical monster from Périgord, condemned to roam the country by night. Legend has it that the *lébérou*, his body swathed in an animal skin, would eat dogs, impregnate village women and jump on the backs of nocturnal walkers, forcing them to carry him. The following morning he would take on the form of a caring neighbour.

'*Lébérou, lébérou!*' the cry was immediately taken up by other villagers. Men made the sign of the cross with their forefingers as if warding off a vampire.

'Prussian, it's your fault we found the Lac Rouge farmer dead at the bottom of his well, with a dog paw in his mouth!'

'Prussian, it's your fault that my brother hanged himself with the halter of his last cow when he came back from burying it!'

'Prussian, it's your fault that I don't know where to get fodder this winter. There's no maize, no beans, nuts or turnips. Scoundrel! Here, take that!'

It's your fault! It's your fault! They blamed Alain for all their woes. The drought, his fault! The problems with Prussia, his fault! His heart, bones, blood, feet and eyelids became a mush, barely held together by pieces of flesh. They were smashing his entire body. The earth of the main street, arid for so long, was joyfully soaking up his blood. Alain was jostled and kicked by clogged feet. He was no longer present; his dilated pupils were vacant. Murguet dragged a fork across Alain's stomach as though he were turning clods of earth. Enough is enough!

There was a crossroads in the town centre. On the left, on the corner of the road leading to Nontron, sprawled the long inn belonging to Élie Mondout, grocer and tobacconist. In painted lettering on the pink-brick façade were the words:

> *Chas Mondout*
> *lu po ei boun,*
> *lu vei ei dou,*
> *la gent benaisé.*

> (At Mondout's,
> the bread is good,
> the wine is sweet,
> the people happy.)

The tables were set with pewter dishes and iron forks, and Élie Mondout's customers sat gawping at Alain. By now he was nothing more than pig or poultry feed.

'Filthy Prussian, take that for my son who you sent to Reichshoffen!'

Piarrouty bashed him once more in the head with his weighing hook and made for the inn, shouting, 'I saw his brains!' He drew vast amounts of water and went to wash his hook, much to Élie Mondout's astonishment.

The innkeeper had been busy rushing to and fro, making soup from leftover meat, slicing ham and bread, cooking up last year's chestnuts, and bringing up demijohns of wine from the cellar. No doubt he hadn't even realised what was happening in the town square behind the kaleidoscope of colourful clothing.

But now, emerging from the kitchen, he was speechless. He found his comfortably seated customers following the spectacle that was unfolding in the thronging inn. People rose in turn to participate in the carnage. Roland Liquoine stamped on Alain's chest, sending pain searing through his heart. A miller with a flail said he was threshing barley, and his ferocious zeal caused Alain even more suffering. Murguet took a swing at Alain's crotch, shouting, 'Snake! Snake!' with unparalleled fury. He roared several times and then sat down. Another man aimed at Alain's face, which was streaming blood. Alain was terrified. The Marthon notary, whom Alain had arranged to see on Bretanges business, pitched in too. Clutching his leather briefcase and wearing a white silk tie, he kicked Alain on his already battered mouth with the tip of his black patent-kid shoes. Lamongie left the table and planted a fork deep in Alain's right eye, blinding him. He then returned to his seat and ordered a carafe of wine from the appalled ashen-faced innkeeper.

'Get away! Get away from my inn, you savages! Get away from here or I'll shoot you!' he said, going off in search of his gun.

'Don't do that, Élie. There are six hundred of them and you can't stop them,' said his wife, waylaying him.

'But we can't let them kill him like that! Where's Anna?'

10

MOUSNIER'S INN

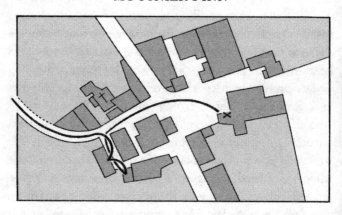

Scared off by the threat of Mondout's blunderbuss, the vast, frenzied mob moved towards the village square. Antony, Mazerat and Dubois hurried over to Alain. They had been forced to skirt round part of the village, until they found Alain being kicked around outside Mousnier's inn. His friends, together with Bouteaudon and the mayor's nephew, picked him up and tried to help him into the inn but the door was banged shut, crushing his hand. Three fingers fell to the floor.

As the door swung back open slightly, Alain used his good eye to scour the inside of the newly restored inn. It was an open room with light wooden beams. He could just hear the ticking of a gold clock standing on the mantelpiece.

The pendulum shone momentarily behind the glass. The wallpaper had a pretty, delicate floral pattern. A picture of Alain's fellow sufferer, Christ crucified on Golgotha, hung on the wall. Alain was facing a looking glass, where he was able to see himself for the first time that day.

His head had become a bloody globe, with death laughing impatiently in his left eye. His face had suffered an avalanche, and was pitted with holes and craters. He was unrecognisable, a pitiful sight. His naked torso was deformed, his whole body twitched. In the mirror's reflection, he could see a man in a straw hat approaching him from behind, armed with a hatchet. It was Jean Brouillet, the owner of the Gaugrilles estate. As boys, he and Alain had built tree houses together. Now, however, a sly Brouillet seemed in a hurry to finish Alain off, even though he had done him no harm. Finally! Alain turned round and focused his remaining eye on the brute, who no longer recognised him.

'Go on, hi' me, hi' me, migh' as well! Go on! Go on!'

Alain's jaw was broken in several places and he was unable to articulate clearly. He awaited the inevitable blow that would perhaps kill him, but Bouteaudon stepped in front of the hatchet.

'Stop, Brouillet! Leave him be!'

Bouteaudon was all the more supportive of Alain since he himself had always been something of an outsider, as millers often are. Mazerat and Dubois came to his aid, pushed Buisson aside and forced the Campot brothers back, while Antony begged Mousnier to let Alain in. But the innkeeper – a man with a weak chin who was wearing a black wide-brimmed felt hat – stood blocking the doorway, and refused.

'You're out of your mind! A Prussian in my inn?' he said, from the entrance.

'He isn't a Prussian, he's Monsieur de Monéys!' retorted Antony angrily.

'Is that so? I don't recognise him,' replied Mousnier, looking at Alain. 'What if he is a Prussian? My newly renovated inn will be destroyed if I let a Prussian in.'

'This young man lent you money for the work, interest free . . .'

'I never borrowed money from a Prussian!'

'Ach! 'Ousnier, iss 'e, A-ain!' protested Alain, trying to force his way in.

'I don't even recognise that voice,' said the innkeeper to Antony. 'He's got a strange accent, he has. I didn't understand a word he said. Was that German?'

And Mousnier slammed the door in Alain's face, leaving him to the mercy of the baying mob. Someone threw a stone that hit the wall to the right of his head. Alain stood hunched, clutching his head in his hands. A mason known to be gregarious and to love dancing – the life and soul of the party – eyed him slyly and smiled. He thought deeply, sure that he could dredge up some vice that would do just as much damage as any shining sword.

'The report that this man wants to send to the government is not a plan to divert the course of the Nizonne! In fact, it's a ludicrous plan to stop people keeping their cows' horns, unless they dress like him!' he sniggered.

'What? Why?'

So it was that this strange tale now spread like wildfire through Hautefaye.

'Who on earth does he think he is? Let's pull off the rest of his clothes and then he'll have to remove his cows' horns too. Strip him! Strip the Prussian!'

They flung themselves at his legs and tore off his trousers. Alain was now completely naked and still being attacked. The torment was unending.

'When the time comes, the Emperor will know who hit him and he will reward everybody. He will pay out!' promised a woodcutter from Fontroubade.

'Really?'

A child aimed a slingshot at Alain's nose.

'Come now,' shouted Antony. 'Surely there are fifty men here who will help us put a stop to this atrocity? Who's with us?'

His pleas went unanswered. Instead, people repeated, 'The Emperor will pay us for doing his work!' They pummelled Alain relentlessly, carefully aiming their clogs at his kidneys, stomach and face. Hautefaye's schoolmaster, whose whiskers were reminiscent of General Cambronne's famous moustache, stood with one hand in the pocket of his white drill trousers. He kicked Alain in the head as though he were kicking a ball. His lower leg was covered in blood. Even he was under the influence of these thugs. At that point, Alain was like a small ship that has lost its mast yet still battles against the storm. He pitched and rolled under powerful eddies of kicks.

'Over there, the corn exchange! There was no corn this year. Let's take him there and quarter him!' bawled the roofer from La Chapelle-Saint-Robert, as though he had just discovered land from the crow's nest.

And so it was that Alain's soul, victim of a terrible shipwreck, prepared to cast off.

11

THE CORN EXCHANGE

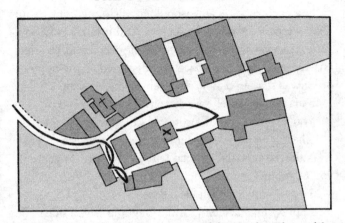

Alain lay on his back, his arms and legs splayed out like a starfish. He was suspended in midair, three feet off the ground. The Campot brothers, Chambort and Mazière had bound his wrists and his huge swollen ankles with ropes, and were pulling him in four different directions. The taut ropes were keeping Alain aloft.

'Heave ho!'

There were shouts of encouragement. When Alain's tormentors pulled, he was raised off the ground and when they slackened their hold, his back – an open wound – hit the tiled floor. Their movements became rhythmic and soon they were off again. Alain rose towards the rafters supporting the tiled roof.

'Heave ho!'

His tormentors sniggered, slithering and sliding in Alain's blood. They started again. Lord, if only it were an amusing game and not an attempt to tear Alain limb from limb. Other men arrived. Soon there were a dozen of them pulling each rope. Alain's shoulders dislocated; his femurs were wrenched from their sockets. Did it hurt? How to be sure? His eyes were wide open yet he seemed to be asleep. His sense of time and space was distorted as the universal order was shattered. The sky itself seemed frozen.

'This is a disgrace!' said Antony's voice from afar.

'You've got no right!' protested Mazerat by his side.

'There's no law and order any more,' came the reply.

'Animals, animals!' sobbed Dubois. 'Where do you think you're going?'

'To wash my hands in his blood.'

Alain swung back and forth depending which side pulled the hardest. When they pulled in unison and the ropes were stretched to their limit, Alain's raised body flapped like a sheet. His blood sprayed everywhere in a mist of tiny droplets. It looked like a constellation. Mingled with the specks of light filtering through the tiled roof, it was a beautiful sight. His blood fell like drizzle as he plummeted towards the tiled floor. He was yanked up once more and all his joints exploded.

The crowd, in their straw hats, smocks, clogs and colourful ribbons, gathered on three sides of the corn exchange to watch. People linked arms to support each other as they swayed back and forth, screaming insults, a harsh tide of cruel words.

The men strained like beasts of burden. Anyone would think they were torturing the man who had attempted to assassinate Louis XV. What was his name? Alain could no longer remember. His mind was gone. They hauled on the ropes. Good God, what strength! Their anger was unjustified and senseless (well, anger always is unjustified and senseless). Alain rose into the air, taking with him his morose concerns. Try not to think about the final plunge.

His healthy blood drained away by the bucketful, spurting from his arteries, forming pools. Jean Campot, at Alain's right foot, slipped in the blood and fell, taking with him everyone on his rope. This sent the group opposite off balance and they toppled backwards. Drunk, the men to the right and left doubled up laughing and let the rope slip between their fingers.

With no one restraining him, Alain jumped up and rushed bleeding out of the hall, leaving a trail of bloody footprints behind him.

12

THE WOOL MERCHANT'S CART

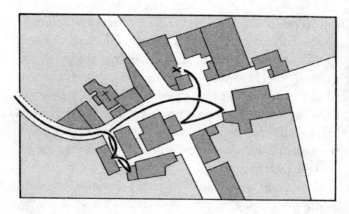

Alain was escaping! People in the corn exchange had believed he was well and truly dead this time, when suddenly he had risen to his feet. The astonished mob, taking him for some kind of ghost, a mythical creature – a *lébérou* for certain – parted in fear, clearing a path for him. He ran with an incredible surge of energy, like a headless chicken. There was no doubt it was a miracle.

His horseshoes grated on the gravel path, and his long shadow formed a strange lolloping silhouette under the burning sun. His outstretched arms were at a strange angle; his shoulders were almost halfway down his chest. His legs were also all askew. His knees rolled in a figure-of-eight movement, something not even seen in the circus. The whole spectacle was terrifying. A howl rattled in his chest like a hurricane whistling through a ruin.

'Catch him! The Prussian's escaping!' yelled Chambort.

Resembling a fallen gargoyle, Alain ran. He mistakenly thought he was on the road to Nontron, but arrived at a dead end, where the wool merchant – Donzeau – had parked his cart. A fatal error – especially since the mob was closing in on him, like a raging army.

Like bloodhounds on his trail, they continued to hurl abuse at him, in a volley of slanderous accusations. Their forked tongues hissed venomous words. Such shameful and disgraceful human behaviour had never been seen before. Enough of this Waterloo! Enough of this mob! He could take no more from his attackers. Enough! Leave him alone!

''Eave 'e! 'Eave 'e!'

He sprang forward – how was this possible? – and grabbed a stake from the wool merchant's cart. He turned to face his pursuers. Naked and covered in blood, shit and wounds, a half-blind amputee, Alain faced the raging horde alone. He was the scion of a long line of Périgord knights and he wanted the family name to live on. Determination burnt in his tearful, throbbing head! His limbs beat the air like wings. He stumbled. His thoughts flitted like bats. Étienne Campot stepped forward and removed the stake from Alain's hands without difficulty, raised it and dealt him a massive blow. Alain keeled over backwards between the shafts of Donzeau's cart, horseshoes waving in the air. His body rolled and finally came to rest under Mercier's wagon.

13

MERCIER'S WAGON

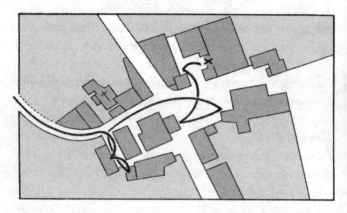

Clogs clattered on the wooden planks, like a spatter of heavy raindrops. Alain lay on the ground, curled in a bleeding ball, eyeing the many feet that were trying to kick him.

He was safe between the wheels of the large horse-drawn carriage parked against a wall. Feet could not reach him there. Men gathered round in ascending circles, banging on the wheels, the suspension, and the planks of the cart, which was used to drive families to funerals and weddings or to take them to Périgueux market.

They stamped up and down in their heavy clogs, the studs in their soles hitting the metal frame and sending up showers of sparks. Their heels came thumping down on the rotting shafts, which splintered. The floor caved in. Between the broken slats, Alain could now see the underside of the seats and the thin upright columns at the four corners of the carriage. The curtains came loose and flew off. It was surreal! Tornadoes of dust glittered in the sunshine.

The carriage, specially decorated for the parades, was like a motorised machine. With pistons and explosions, it seemed to be turning into an automobile and moving all by itself. Wait, no, men were pushing it. Buisson and Mazière hauled Alain out by his legs. His head dragged behind, bumping on the stones. He was back in Hautefaye village square once more. Bernard Mathieu appeared, sporting his mayor's sash, jiggling the tassels and fringes.

'Hey, Moureau, don't you think he's had enough?' he asked the old farmer from Grand-Gillou, who was pelting Alain with stones.

'But, Your Worship, he's a Prussian. He must pay the price!'

The old farmer's reply was met with cheers of 'Prussian! Villain! Villain!' The men surrounding Alain laughed and boasted, playing up their horrific behaviour to impress each other. Look how many of them supported Napoleon III. They weren't fooled by a Prussian except . . . Alain was no Prussian. But he no longer had the strength to contradict them. Battered and weary of the constant attacks, the gratuitous jibes, he let them drag him along without putting up the slightest resistance.

Some of his attackers were tired as well. They could be seen wandering around, dishevelled and clutching bloodstained sticks. 'Hitting a man for two hours is exhausting!' They left to have a drink.

Despite Alain's cordial greeting earlier, they did not

even deign to say goodbye. He could not endure any more, but his few friends still did not desert him. Brutal hands continued to pummel him and his situation became ever more desperate. Antony shouted at Bernard Mathieu – a good-for-nothing king presiding over an execution.

'Your Worship, rather than putting on airs and strutting around in your sash, help us save him! A terrible crime is being committed in your village!'

'Why are you meddling?'

'I'm meddling because someone is being murdered and you're doing nothing!'

'Get this man out of here,' the mayor ordered the men holding Alain's ankles, taking a step towards them. 'He's blocking the road. Take him somewhere else.'

Antony sighed in despair.

'What shall we do with him somewhere else?' enquired Buisson and Mazière.

'Whatever you want!' replied the mayor, completely out of his depth. 'Eat him if you like.'

14

THE WHEELBARROW

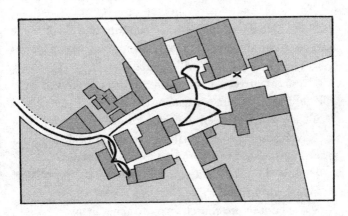

Well, to think that Alain was deemed to have a weak constitution by the medical board! He did not know why he was still alive, but his heart continued to flutter in his chest. The people towing him turned to the right, towards whatever fate awaited him.

'Burn him! Roast him!'

'Burn him! If not, the Prussians will come and set us alight!' urged the villagers, hoping to ward off the spectre of a fire.

'After shoeing him like an ox, we'll cook him like a pig!'

'He needs to be plucked before we cook him!' proposed a raucous female voice that sounded familiar.

The mob paused to think. A large group went in search of

wood – branches, planks and broken furniture. They tossed it onto Alain's chest with needless brutality. He had become a wheelbarrow – his legs the shaft and his head the wheel.

'Take the Prussian over there, where the firewood is!'

They also needed some straw and a means of lighting the fire.

'Hey, Thibassou, here's one sou. Run and fetch some matches from Mousnier's inn and bring some newspaper as well. The *Dordogne Echo* will do fine!'

Chambort arrived with a bale of straw, followed by a villager yelling at him for stealing his fodder.

'That's worth thirteen sous, you know!'

'Never fear. Napoleon III will pay you back for your straw bale because we're using it to save France!'

'I know the mayor's a coward but where's the priest?' cried Mazerat from afar.

'Passed out in the church from drinking in an attempt to avert this disaster. He's snoring at Christ's feet,' boomed Bouteaudon's voice.

Mazière and Buisson dragged Alain along by his legs. Bumping on the ground, his head oozed a long trail of brains and blood. The tragic carnival was reaching its climax. The villagers had destroyed his body and now they were going to burn it. Alain was going to the theatre of hell. He was nothing more than a rag doll, and burning him would mark the end of the festivities.

He was driven out of the village on a tidal wave of abuse. Menacing river banks closed in on him, echoing with baying voices. Memories of profoundly happy, peaceful occasions from his comfortable former existence came rushing back.

Alain had fallen from grace and was now being dragged by his ankles towards the fairground. The murder that the crowd was about to commit was a declaration of love for France. People hurled chestnut branches onto Alain's chest, onto the man they saw as a human wheelbarrow, all the while shouting 'Long live the Emperor!' Alain endured their blows without much struggle. They hauled him along the path to a place that seemed to be a rubbish tip. They had arrived at the dried-up lake, where each year a bonfire was lit on midsummer's night.

15

THE DRIED-UP LAKE

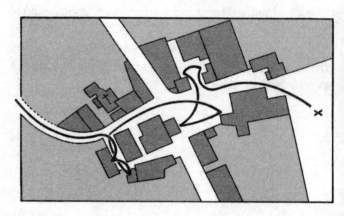

Mazière, Buisson and the younger Campot brother came to help the other men, and they dumped Alain's body on the dried-up lake bed. The water had evaporated after months of searing heat. Alain lay on his back on the parched, cracked earth, his head turned slightly to one side. He was still breathing slightly.

'Hooray! He's not dead! He's not dead! We're going to burn him alive!'

Alain had been dreaming of a quick and easy death. Or rather, he had been praying for it. He heard the voice of his childhood friend Chambort – now a blacksmith in Pouvrières – organising the construction of the funeral pyre. Alain had known him so well; how could his old friend have turned against him so suddenly?

'Bring more wood; bring vine shoots and cartwheels, and pull up the fence posts!'

They had now reached the fringes of the livestock fair. Chambort spread straw over his former playmate's chest. Alain could still move his left foot. He wanted to escape. Chestnut branches and planks were piled on top of him. Alain still needed to go and buy a heifer for Bertille. He pushed at the heap of wood with his fingers, but Chambort jumped on him.

'Trample on the pyre to make a good fire!'

Chambort stood on the vine shoots and packed down the wood with his feet. He waddled around, putting on airs. He trampled the wretched Alain underfoot from his makeshift platform.

'Long live the Emperor!' he called. 'Long live the Empress and the young imperial Prince!'

Some cattle farmers and horse traders who had been at the far side of the fair all afternoon were oblivious to what had been happening. They were astounded to see a pyre being erected atop a fellow human being.

'They've caught a Prussian and they're going to burn him! War has reached Hautefaye!' shouted some in a panic, hurrying along their cattle and getting away from the fair as quickly as possible.

'We must go to Nontron and tell the police!' said a farmer's wife, losing her headdress as she raced downhill, prodding her heifer's rump into a gallop.

Some visitors, having grasped the situation more clearly, were appalled by the mob's brutality and cradled their heads in their hands. Many, mesmerised, watched what followed. Chambort descended from the pyre.

'The youngest should light the fire,' he decided, 'just like on midsummer's night. Come closer, children. Hey, you there, what's your name?'

'Pierre Delage, but people call me 'Poleon,' replied a young boy of five with bruised bare feet who was clinging to his mother's threadbare skirt.

'His father gave him that nickname after the Emperor,' she explained, 'when he returned from fighting the Russians in the Crimea.'

'Very good. And where is your heroic husband?'

'He died in the Battle of Forbach.'

'Really?' said Chambort, looking pained. 'Then come, Napoleon, set this Prussian alight. The Emperor will send you a medal and some shoes.'

'Shoes? Go on,' said the poor mother to her child.

'Don't do it, Pierre!' shouted Dubois and Georges Mathieu.

'If you do, the police will put you in prison!' added Antony and Bouteaudon.

'Don't do it!' yelled Mazerat.

The villagers turned and chased Alain's protectors away. The child hesitated, but Jean Campot lit a match and held it out to him.

'Come on, Napoleon, burn the pig . . .'

The child knelt to light the paper, but he couldn't keep the flame alive. The match went out too quickly; he had to start again. Alain could smell the wood. A third match sparked near one of his ears and the *Dordogne Echo* caught fire, the flames spreading quickly to the straw and the vine shoots. He tossed about beneath the conifer branches. Logs blazed and the smell of resin hung in the air. Alain still appeared to be moving behind the curtains of fire as they sprang up.

Alain watched the hazy crowd dance through the yellow and orange waves, throwing their hats and sticks up to the sky. A low, regular drone like a beehive filled the air.

'Long live the Emperor!' coughed the mayor, still sporting his sash, as he inhaled a cloud of smoke.

The men found killing a human being just as easy as harvesting their crops, and they danced and spun in circles. Alain was still alive and his heavy breathing sounded like air escaping a bellows. The end was nigh. His hair smouldered, his chest caught fire. He was finding it harder and harder to breathe. A woman was yelling wildly. It was the schoolmaster's wife, her treacherous red lips drawn back in a grimace, revealing her fangs. Near her stood Anna – the girl whose hand Alain would have liked to hold as he watched their child playing in the vineyard. She gazed at him, weeping, and mouthed a sentence he could not hear. It seemed she was promising him something. Her look fuelled the flames round Alain's heart and it burst from his shattered chest. One crazed yet dreamy eye remained open.

His ashes floated towards the blue sky, a sky that sang and called to him. He left the pleasures of this world, victim of a misunderstanding that could not have had a more gruesome outcome. His ashes finally rose above the fathomless world of fools and the depravity of these people, guilty of a crime beyond their comprehension. His flesh was now roasting in its own juice. It was a wretched end. Several people asked,

'Who was he?' They had spent all afternoon massacring a man without even enquiring who he was.

'We're cooking a fine pig!'

Alain had become a spit roast. The skin on his thighs and shoulders crackled and blistered, swelling with bubbles full of boiling fat. They burst and a glistening, even appetising juice spurted out.

'It would be a shame to waste this fat!' said Besse ruefully. 'Does anybody want to try it?'

A mother took a six-pound loaf of bread from her basket and sliced it up. With a spatula, she scooped up some of the fat pooling near Alain's elbows and spread it on the bread, distributing it to her children.

'Eat up! Eat up, darlings. It's not every day you get something on your bread these days. Blow on it. It's hot.'

More slices of bread dripping with scalding human fat were passed around, and good men wolfed them down.

'What does it taste of?'

'A bit like veal.'

People started flocking towards Alain's remains for a slap-up feast. Everyone gave an opinion, sounding like great culinary experts.

'It would taste better washed down with a little glass of white Pontignac.'

Alain could never have imagined they would say such things about him, the deputy mayor of Beaussac. His ashes rose higher, swirling around in the air above the crowd who were feasting as they did on the most important holidays. They devoured their cannibal sandwiches. Anna saw Thibassou take a mouthful and wash it down with white wine. Eating this body would purge the community. Small satisfied burps mingled with the sounds of chewing. It was a joy to hear. Boiling fat caused overhasty lips to blister.

'Ouch!'

'He burnt you! He's still hurting you.'

A heavy, acrid smoke hung above the dried-up lake, rising slowly. Families danced and children squalled. Unmarried men continued drinking and eyed the charred body that the fire had transformed. Like clouds in the sky or logs in the fireplace, the body changed according to where the person was standing.

'Look, he resembles a wild boar. What do you think?'

'A bird.'

'Those two embers glowing side by side look like Beelzebub's eyes. You can see his yellow tongue flickering.'

Everybody saw their own personal demons appear. They stood there mesmerised, like children.

'A stag!'

He was no longer a man. Madame Lachaud delivered a sharp blow between the legs of his charred remains with a spade. His chest split open to reveal a dazzling interior. Fire tongs in hand, she continued rummaging around inside. Her husband started to worry.

'What are you looking for?'

'His treasures. Ah look, look, his nuts!'

Madame Lachaud's proud husband observed her passing Alain's testicles from one hand to the other to cool them down. He found her devilish attitude amusing.

'You wouldn't . . .'

Perverse like no other, she did as she pleased and munched

them defiantly, staring at Anna. She bit down hard. With her bodice open and her voluminous breasts glistening with sweat, she looked like a rabid dog. From between the jaws of the victim's burnt skull, big bubbles emerged and popped noisily, giving her a fright.

'What's that Prussian gibbering about now?'

'He's saying: "I'd love to fuck you, but my cock's burning",' translated her husband.

Around them, people roared with laughter. A man takes a long time to burn. On the horizon, the setting sun was weeping blood. The scene was grisly. The ashes from Alain's charred corpse were dispersed in all directions by the wind. They slipped under the soles of the men who were leaving as they wiped their greasy mouths contentedly on their sleeves.

'There are too many Prussians in Lorraine to put up with one in our village! This one's burning. I think we've made an example of him.'

'I'm glad I hit him in the face four times with my stick, and that those blows really counted against that de Monéys.'

'Against who?'

'Against the Prussian.'

'Oh yes, me too. I whacked the Prussian too.'

'You missed a wonderful roast!' they told everyone they met. 'He had as much fat as three sows, that Prussian. He would have lasted us the whole week!'

The ratter retched on hearing all the culinary details.

'Oh, don't act all high and mighty!' laughed the cannibals. 'You eat rats, and old ones at that!'

'But that was Monsieur de Monéys.'

'What?'

As they exhaled, fatty residue landed on men's shoulders. The burnt remains of Magdeleine-Louise and Amédée de Monéys's son floated up in the air and drifted southwards. The moon gave off an oppressive light that night. Falling leaves whirled and sparred on the path that led to Bretanges. A young man carrying a lantern ran in the direction of the distant house. A frail mother stood at the open drawing-room window worrying about her son. Even though it was dark, the heat was still suffocating. She closed the lid of the piano and saw a plume of smoke rising up over Hautefaye. The sound of running footsteps was like a downpour on the dust. It was their servant, Pascal.

'Why is he running so fast when it's so hot?' wondered Alain's mother, in surprise.

'Madame de Monéys! Madame de Monéys!'

Pascal burst into the seventeenth-century house.

'It's Alain, he's been . . .'

A terrible scream tore through the countryside and the night.

16

THE NEXT DAY

A large hand with stubby fingers unceremoniously prodded the stomach of an inert recumbent figure, an extremely fragile white statue whose features were frozen in an imploring expression.

'Oh, forgive me! I'm very sorry!' exclaimed the doctor, hastily withdrawing his hand.

'Grim,' muttered his assistant, taking from his satchel a notebook and quill, which he dipped in ink. His fingers poised, he added, 'I'm ready, Dr Roby-Pavillon.'

The portly doctor, who was also mayor of Nontron, rubbed his palms together, sending up a cloud of ash like rice powder. He wiped his hands on his clothes, leaving white smears on his black trousers.

'We are no longer of the same clay, Monsieur de Monéys,' sighed the doctor, sadly.

His voice echoed through Hautefaye's small church, where Alain's charred remains had been carefully transferred. Alain lay on a white sheet draped over the altar. It was lit by several church candles, and others from the grocer, Élie Mondout, their flames flickering in the dim light of mournful day. A ray of sunlight shone through the stained-glass window and danced prettily over Alain's neck and shoulders, like a brightly coloured scarf, a tiny, unexpected delight.

The victim of the execution, carried out by means abolished centuries earlier, lay on the slab. Silence reigned, shattered only by the doctor's stentorian voice dictating the autopsy report to his assistant.

'The body is almost entirely burnt and is lying on its back.'

The doctor had a trim beard and a round head of tight curls. He walked around the altar and examined Alain's remains, giving a meticulous description.

'The face is turned slightly to the left, and the lower limbs are extended. The right hand is missing three fingers and is raised in supplication.'

Occasionally the doctor stumbled over an empty bottle which rolled noisily over the flagstones. The whole place smelt of wine, and the fragrance of incense mingled with the stench of vomit. The doctor's shoes crunched on broken glass.

'The left hand sits on the corresponding shoulder, the fingers splayed as though begging for mercy.' Alain's facial features were frozen in an expression of agony, his twisted torso thrown back. The flames had captured Alain's dying moments and preserved them as evidence.

A groan emanated from elsewhere in the church. It was the priest, disturbed by the doctor's loud voice. His cassock somewhat the worse for wear, the priest was sitting in a pew, elbows on his knees, head in his hands, nursing an awful headache. The Norman arches had witnessed unheard-of goings-on the day before, and the priest was now hung over. It was bad enough that the pinewood statue of Christ was being eaten away by dry rot, sprinkling the floor with dust. 'Keep your voice down,' the priest ordered the doctor, who continued to dictate his report.

'Having examined the victim's corpse, it is reasonable to conclude firstly that Monsieur de Monéys was burnt alive. Secondly, his death was caused by burns and asphyxiation. Thirdly, the recorded injuries on the corpse were caused by pointed, sharp and blunt instruments while he was still alive. Fourthly, one of the injuries, a blow to the head, was delivered from behind the victim while he was still standing. Fifthly, Monsieur de Monéys was dragged along while he was still alive. Sixthly, the combination of his injuries would inevitably have led to his death. Signed in Hautefaye, on 17 August 1870, by Dr Roby-Pavillon, physician.'

The portly doctor turned round. His shoes squeaked, causing the priest to wince. He was having trouble sobering up from the day before. His complexion was literally green and he was close to vomiting. Just then the bronze church bells struck nine, ringing out over Hautefaye.

Police on horseback had combed the surrounding countryside and were now returning to the village. They had arrested several men, who plodded behind them, attached to ropes, hands bound and heads bowed. They were escorted to the already crowded village square and left there. The police officers then set off again in search of other culprits on all the farms and in all the shops in the area.

The public prosecutor from Bordeaux, a young man with sideburns, who had arrived at dawn, had a word with one of the sergeants.

'Take it easy! Don't bring back too many. We can't lock them all up! There are only twenty-one cells in Périgueux jail, and the court won't be able to try that many either. Think about it. Do you realise that you'd have to arrest six hundred people? It's a . . . most unusual crime.'

The prosecutor removed his glasses, wiped them and put them back on as though he could not quite believe his eyes.

'Very well,' replied the sergeant. 'But should we arrest the first man who knocked out his teeth with an iron bar, for example?'

'No, why? You'll see there are so many people who did worse . . . Just settle for the main perpetrators.'

'And the man who gouged out his eye with a fork?'

'Yes, well . . . the man who gouged out his eye, if you like. But don't worry too much, we've got enough. Is that the prefect of Ribérac's carriage I spy behind those trees?'

'Yes, that's him.'

'The whole of Périgord is deeply concerned,' said the prefect, alighting from his carriage.

Hautefaye was still in a state of shock as it began to stir. It was almost as though the entire village was hung over. The fierce beauty of the surrounding countryside seemed to beg the question 'What on earth did you do yesterday? What came over you?' The villagers shuddered again, appalled at themselves. 'What did come over us?' Confusion and bewilderment reigned. Apart from the main square, the village was deserted, almost abandoned. It was in a state of numbness. Residents stayed at home, hiding behind drawn curtains. Sitting around helplessly behind locked doors, eyes staring blankly, mouths hanging open.

'Open up! It's the police!' Fists rapped on the doors.

'What have we done?'

A surveyor was pacing up and down Hautefaye's narrow lanes, taking measurements. The taste of slow poison and the smell of death still lingered in the air. He took some tobacco from a pig's-bladder pouch and stuffed it into his pipe. The surveyor then took out a notebook and sat in the blazing sun marking off the various stations at which Alain had stopped during his ordeal, and plotted a map of his zigzag progress through the village.

Journalists in elegant, grey loose-fitting coats and felt hats hurried over to the prefect, who was donning a cocked hat sporting a large ostrich feather. They followed him to the little lane by Bernard Mathieu's house, which was surrounded by drummers, scarlet uniforms and black horses.

'To Alain, who died in God's love,' intoned the priest above the roll of goatskin drums. Still nursing his headache, he was now alone in the church.

The elderly mayor of Hautefaye descended the steps of his house wearing just a vest and a somewhat stained and crumpled tricolour sash. He must have slept in it. Above his head, a police officer was perched on a ladder, taking the French flag down from his house. Several men emerged carrying registers of births, marriages and deaths, jostling Bernard Mathieu as they passed.

'Where shall we take them?'

'To Mousnier's place,' the mayor suggested. 'They knew Alain very well.'

The alarmed prefect shook his head.

'Ah yes, I forgot!' the mayor continued. 'Well, take them to the schoolmaster. Madame Lachaud was very fond of Monsieur de Monéys . . .'

'Clearly, you were elected mayor by virtue of your age alone,' said the prefect, raising his eyes to the heavens. His voice was cold and harsh. 'Gentlemen,' he ordered, 'take these registers to Élie Mondout's inn. He shall assume the mayor's duties for the time being.'

The prefect then drew his gleaming sword. The moment of reckoning had arrived. He slid the sword under Bernard Mathieu's tricolour sash and gave it a violent tug. Bernard Mathieu bit his lip. Everybody was expecting him to say something, but there was a lump in his throat and no words came out. He farted.

'Wait, that's not what I meant!'

Élie Mondout's inn had become the investigating magistrate's chambers. Men of the law sat at tables and ordered the country folk with their ragged clothes smelling of manure and garlic to parade before them. They had been reported by Antony, Mazerat, Dubois and the rest of Alain's protectors, who were present at the inn. Élie Mondout tried to recall the names of the customers who had been sitting outside the day before.

'There was Roland Liquoine, Girard Feytou, Murguet, Lamongie, the Marthon notary. Who else was here? There were so many of them . . .'

The accused entered the inn, awkward and disconcerted at finding themselves under arrest. Thibassou came in flanked by two gendarmes, his hands bound. The boy was rather proud to be considered a man and treated as such. He was oblivious of the error of his ways and confidently met people's eyes. Anna was slicing bread and serving drinks.

'I was the one who squealed,' she said, walking past him. She gazed at him sadly and then closed her eyes. She opened them again and stared straight at him.

'You animal!' she spat with sheer hatred.

She left the room and headed for the kitchen. She did not speak, smile or sing as she worked. She was just a shadow, slowly going through the routine of getting out plates and cutlery. She stopped dead in the middle of her tasks and then went back to preparing a simple meal of cod and chestnuts.

Soon, through the small window that opened onto the countryside, she heard the pounding of horses' hooves on the dry earth as they dragged away the two prison wagons.

17

THE TRIAL

'Raise your right hand and say "I do solemnly swear".'

'I do solemnly swear, and long live the Emperor!'

'What emperor?'

'Er, that 'Poleon . . . that heaven-sent envoy, Napoleon III!'

'There is no longer an emperor in France.'

'What?'

'He surrendered at the Battle of Sedan on 2 September and was captured. France was declared a republic on 4 September.'

'What?'

'You haven't heard?'

'Well, no . . . News takes a long time to reach us out here in the country, and now that we're in prison . . .'

'The crime you are charged with took place under the Second Empire, but you will be tried by the Third Republic.'

'Oh, I see.'

'You seem miles away. Can you tell me what date it is today, François Chambort?'

'Not really. It's winter, isn't it? I saw snow falling through my cell window.'

'It is 13 December 1870. This is the last of three days of deliberations here in Périgueux criminal court. A verdict will be reached shortly and then you will learn your sentence.'

'I see.'

'You could at least have had a haircut!' called a member of the public.

'Silence! Or I shall have to clear the court,' ordered the judge.

The judge was a fair man. He sat on a raised chair behind a green baize desk, his long sleeves hiding the armrests. The desk was stacked with papers and weighty law tomes. In front of the desk was a small table displaying various exhibits – whips, bloodstained sticks, a ragman's hook, pebbles stained with human fat.

Chambort stood in the witness box, looking awkward in front of a full courthouse. As a blacksmith, he was much more at home handling oxen and horses and beating iron. He was squeezed into his Sunday best and had dark circles under his eyes. He stared intently at the floor.

'What was your relationship to Alain de Monéys?' the judge asked.

'He was a childhood friend and was the kindest man you could ever meet. No, I'm serious – I don't understand what came over me. It's awful, just awful. I'm sickened by what I've done.'

'But you still . . . ?'

'I lost my head.'

'What happened?'

'I let myself get carried away.'

'What can you tell us about the victim?'

'He always thought of others, he was a good man.'

'Yes, he certainly tasted good!' said a mocking voice from the public gallery.

'Death to the cannibals!' shouted others. 'Leave him to us! We'll show him justice!'

The judge banged his gavel on the desk and looked out at the sea of furious faces.

'François Chambort,' he continued, 'did you torture Alain de Monéys?'

'Yes, I shoed him and I threw straw on him. I got carried away by the excitement of the mad mob attacking Alain.'

'And you decided to end it all with an *auto-da-fé*?'

'I don't understand that word.'

'Did you help build the funeral pyre?'

'I don't remember.'

'The jury will consider your case. Return to the dock.'

Chambort obeyed, his legs weak.

'No mercy for those monsters!' booed the assembly.

Convinced he would have the support of the already emotional audience, the prosecutor rose, his gown fluttering.

'Send them to the guillotine, Your Honour!' he shouted, red-faced and almost frothing at the mouth.

While the judge's cross-examination had been rather formal, the prosecutor's summing up was nothing of the kind. He spewed epithets as he excoriated Chambort.

'Never was there a more despicable man! There are no words to describe such an individual and I am at a loss to express the horror I feel.'

This was the prosecutor's crowning argument, and he concluded by calling for the maximum penalty – death.

In response to this swooping attack, a stooped, weasel-like lawyer ventured, 'My client has no previous convictions!' in an attempt to retrieve the hopeless situation. 'Anyway, all the accused – villagers, craftsmen – were upstanding citizens prior to this terrible day. That's why this case is so unique. It's not a common-law crime. Something must have triggered the mob's behaviour and—'

'That's enough!' interrupted the judge. 'Speeches for the defence and summings up will be heard later, before the jury retires to deliberate. I call the next witness.'

The next man entered the witness box, wearing a stiff green jacket that was very coarse and very ugly. He was also wearing a woollen scarf, socks and clogs.

'First name, surname, profession?' asked the judge.

'Antoine Léchelle, farmer.'

'Describe what happened on 16 August.'

'The sky fell on our heads.'

'Why did you kill Monsieur de Monéys?'

'Because people were saying that he'd shouted "Long live Prussia!"'

'Yet he had actually enlisted to go and fight the Prussians.'

'Really? No one mentioned it.'

'*He* did.'

The courtroom walls were covered in a wallpaper with a faint undulating pattern, evoking ocean waves. Everyone was foundering and Antoine Léchelle himself was carried by the tide. He wept over his washed-up life and left the witness box. The next man was mopping his brow.

'François Mazière, you are accused of several acts of barbarity towards Alain de Monéys.'

'People were saying that he was a Prussian and should pay the price. I'd never seen a Prussian and wanted to see one close up.'

'Did you not then notice he was not a Prussian, but in fact your neighbour?'

'He was unrecognisable. His head was covered in blood. You wouldn't have recognised your own mother in that situation, Your Honour!'

'You dragged him by the feet, still alive, to his funeral pyre.'

'Regrettably I did.'

'Earlier, you forced him into the smithy, where he was shod and his toes amputated.'

'I was holding him down, but it was the mob that attacked him.'

'You did too!' shouted Antony from the gallery.

'I did too? Well, we must all have lost our reason that day.'

As the witnesses testified one by one, they hunched their shoulders and hung their heads in shame. They all said the same thing: 'We don't know what came over us.' It was the same story every time. Nobody said anything against the victim or suggested that he was in any way to blame.

'Mathieu Murguet, did you use a fork to turn over Alain de Monéys's stomach the way you turn over earth? Did you do such a heinous thing?'

'Regrettably I did.'

Demoralised, the accused shrank into themselves, exhausted by the legal jargon, which was like a foreign language to them.

'Why this orgy of violence?'

Piarrouty looked like the living dead. His skin was ashen and his eyes were vacant.

'We went mad,' declared Buisson. 'Of course de Monéys was a good man.'

'We acted like children,' said Besse. 'I think we were even dreaming at one point. When he was burning, I thought I saw a pig and Piarrouty swears he saw arms cradling a baby. Lamongie saw a bird. Liquoine said, "He looks like Beelzebub. You can see his yellow tongue flickering".'

18

THE VERDICT

Dordogne Criminal Court
(Special Session)
Presided by Judge Brochon, justice of the Bordeaux
Court of Appeal

The Hautefaye affair
Murder of Alain de Monéys

Twenty-one men stood accused.

*On 13 December 1870, at seven o'clock in the evening, the
High Court reached a verdict on those accused of the Hautefaye
murder.*

The following were sentenced:

*Pierre **Buisson**, François **Chambort**, François **Léonard**
(known as Piarrouty) and François **Mazière** – death penalty.*

The execution will take place in Hautefaye village square.

*Jean **Campot** – hard labour for life.*

*Étienne **Campot** – eight years' hard labour.*

*Pierre **Besse** – six years' hard labour.*

*Jean **Beauvais**, Jean **Frédérique**, Léonard **Lamongie**,*

*Antoine **Léchelle**, Mathieu **Murguet**, Pierre **Sarlat** — five years' hard labour.*

*Jean **Sallat** (known as Old Moureau) — five years' imprisonment, in consideration of his age (sixty-two).*

*Jean **Brouillet**, Pierre **Brut**, Girard **Feytou**, Roland **Liquoine**, François **Sallat**, accused of the lesser offence of actual bodily harm — one year's imprisonment.*

*Thibault **Limay** (known as Thibassou) has been cleared, in consideration of his age (fourteen) and that he acted rashly, but he shall be sent to a reform institution until he reaches his twentieth birthday.*

*Pierre **Delage** (known as 'Poleon), having acted rashly, is acquitted due to his age (five) and he is granted his freedom.*

19

THE EXECUTION

'There aren't many people. Less than a hundred, I reckon.'

'I could have sworn there were more on the day of the fair . . . I can't see Alain's parents. Didn't they want to come?'

'Didn't you hear? His mother died of grief last autumn. On 31 October, I believe.'

'What about his father?'

'He has sold off the Bretanges estate, all two hundred acres, and put the house up for sale too. He's left the area. He didn't really want to keep bumping into the men who murdered and ate his son.'

The two men hopped up and down in the snow and rubbed their arms in an attempt to keep warm.

'Brr! You can tell it's 6 February. It was much warmer here on 16 August. Did you know they're going to demolish the village?'

'What, destroy Hautefaye?'

'The government is seriously thinking about wiping the village from the map.'

Daybreak came, and with it a feeling of subdued anxiety. The moon was still visible. It unveiled half of its hypocritical face, feigning pity.

'Shall we go closer to the horrible contraption?' suggested one of the men. 'I've not seen one before.'

'It's very rare that they bring a guillotine to the scene of the crime.'

Four pine coffins, their bases covered in sawdust, stood by the guillotine where the executioner was talking to his assistants. The lids were placed to one side. A whistle of metal followed by a solid thud made the two men jump. The executioner had asked his assistant to raise the blade by pulling on the rope and was checking that it fell correctly. The prosecutor took a watch from his waistcoat pocket.

'Seven twenty-five; are you ready?'

The executioner, who was wearing a top hat, nodded.

'Attention!' barked a moustachioed captain. His order was followed by the sound of heels clicking in the pale dawn light. One hundred gendarmes formed a stalwart line from the door of Mousnier's inn to the corn exchange. Behind them came stifled sobs from friends and relatives of the condemned men and from wives wearing black woollen shawls. The door of the renovated inn opened.

Piarrouty was the first to emerge from Mousnier's establishment, which had acted as a temporary jail before the execution. A boy slipped between two gendarmes and held out a cup of coffee. The prosecutor nodded his assent. The ragman drained the cup slowly and then handed it back to the child, gazing at him as though he were his own son.

'My boy, be good and never behave as I did. If ever you feel the urge to hit your neighbour, just throw away your axe and be on your way.'

A few seconds later and Piarrouty's steaming blood could

be seen on the block. In a way, it was as though everyone in the village had been executed. Shutters were closed around the square, but there was still the feeling that, behind the blinds, people were pressing their faces to the windowpanes. Now it was Buisson's turn.

'None of my family is here? Are they still disgusted with me?'

'I will talk to your wife and children,' said the priest, who was supporting him.

'Tell them I'm a swine and I'm sorry for what I did.'

Buisson's head rolled into the basket of sawdust, on top of Piarrouty's, and Mazière soon joined them. He had died whimpering, *'Maman, Maman,'* like an injured nightingale.

'We were once good people, you know,' sighed Chambort.

A large dappled horse with steaming nostrils pulled a cart carrying the four sealed coffins to a communal grave in the cemetery. Drummers, scarlet uniforms and black horses were gathered in front of the corn exchange. Élie Mondout's inn filled rapidly. Each table ordered several drinks, which were promptly served, but on this freezing February morning, people were feeling hungry as well.

'What's there to eat?'

'To eat? Well, there's still some barley soup of course!' replied Élie Mondout. 'Anna, pour the drinks, cut the bread, fill the plates! Anna!'

The executioner's assistant was asking a gaunt-looking Anna for a tub of hot water to wash his clothes in. Her teeth started chattering uncontrollably.

Inside the inn, people talked about the police wagons carrying the men sentenced to hard labour that had left for

La Rochelle and then onto Nou Island in New Caledonia.

'Where's New Caledonia?'

A cattle farmer wondered aloud whether France's most peaceful village had been permanently sullied. Subsequently, people moved on to a rather confused political 'debate'.

'Where's Anna?' asked Élie Mondout.

'Not in the kitchen, nor down in the cellar fetching wine. We would have seen her if she'd left though,' replied his wife. Élie Mondout opened the small back door and surveyed the surrounding countryside.

'Anna! Anna!'

The innkeeper stood at the door, bellowing. His shouts and the rush of air from the open door created a gust that carried off a fleck of ash that had perhaps been there since the previous summer.

'Anna! Anna!'

20

THE NIZONNE MARSHES

Anna lay face down in the snow – dead.

'She was there all along, on the frozen marshes of the Nizonne. No wonder it took you so long to find her . . .'

Dr Roby-Pavillon walked round the dead girl, footsteps crunching in the snow. He was followed by a distraught Élie Mondout and the villager who had discovered her.

'One of my cows got out and I wanted to check she hadn't got stuck near the river.'

The pathologist crouched down, sliding a professional hand under the girl's heavy jacket.

'She was six months pregnant,' he diagnosed.

'What?' gasped Anna's uncle, horrified.

'I wonder if that has anything to do with what's written here,' mused the doctor, straightening up and wiping his hands on his black trousers encrusted with snow.

'I can't read. What does it say?' asked the villager, going over to the giant letters drawn in the snow.

The twenty-three-year-old girl who had once ironed clothes in Angoulême lay still, her head to one side. She wore a thick woollen dress and clumsy hobnail shoes. Lying there, deathly pale and with crystals of frost on her eyelashes, her beautiful lips parted, she looked as if she were simply asleep.

The conscience of the cannibal village, Anna lay on the frozen grass, which had been completely flattened. The louring sky cast a grey mist over the snow. Near Anna's mouth and frozen index finger were written the words 'I love you'.

'I love you? But who's that for? I never saw her look at any boy except Alain de . . .' said Élie Mondout, dumbfounded.

'It looks like one of the magic mirrors the tinkers take from their suitcases,' said the villager, entranced.

'Six months, you say, Doctor?' asked the dead girl's uncle, counting backwards. 'February, January, December . . . She would have conceived mid-August?'

'That's right.'

'But who by? It can't have been the day of the . . .'

'And how did she learn to write?' asked the villager, walking around the letters and admiring them upside-down.

'The schoolmaster's wife taught her,' replied Élie Mondout hollowly.

The villager continued his orbit, finding himself looking at the letters the right way up.

'Either way, the words are big enough to be visible from heaven.'

A speck of ash fluttered down, seemingly from the clouds, and landed on Anna's frosted lip, melting there like a kiss. The doctor and the innkeeper exchanged glances.

'No, it's impossible! How could he have done it? It was that very day, you know!' exclaimed Élie Mondout.

'But he was kept otherwise occupied by everybody else!'

agreed the doctor.

'It's the *lébérou*!' cried the villager, as if in a trance. 'Under the evil spell, his body wrapped in an animal skin, he probably jumped on the girl's back, got her pregnant, and then took on the shape of an innocent neighbouring villager. We need to find out who it is – which one of us – and really show him, show that Prussian what we're made of. With sticks and . . . ! Oh, I swear . . . !'

The mayor of Nontron gazed at the little ripples of the Nizonne and the blue roofs of Hautefaye. Standing wistfully at the water's edge, he listened to the song of the gorse and the reeds.

EPILOGUE

On arrival at the prison camp on Nou Island, the men sentenced to hard labour for the Hautefaye murder were given nicknames by other convicts. There was 'Lamb chop', 'Well cooked', 'Medium rare', 'Grilled steak' and more. Jean Campot was given Alain's surname and soon became accustomed to it. After thirty years of hard labour, he was released for good conduct. He stayed in New Caledonia and had children with a Kanak woman, who took the surname de Monéys as well.

On 16 August 1970, descendants of the de Monéys and the killers' families held a mass to commemorate the hundredth anniversary of the event, which they all attended together. The mass was celebrated in Hautefaye's church – the village had not been wiped off the map after all.

Alain de Monéys's project to divert the Nizonne was accomplished and, one hundred and fifty years on, the region is still thriving as a result.